# Harvest Blessings

## A Small Town Romance Novel

## by Christina Lorenzen

Christina Lorenzen

ISBN-10:1-944203-65-6

ISBN-13:978-1-944203-65-8

# Chapter One

Tacy Clark turned the key in the ignition again, this time holding it a few seconds longer. It was no use. The engine sounded like a tired old appliance, whining and grumbling, refusing to start. Staring at the cup of tea sitting in the cup holder between the front seats, she wished she hadn't stopped but instead gone straight to Aunt Ruby's house. She could have saved herself the buck seventy five and a tow to the house. Now she had two choices - she could hoof the rest of the way to her aunt's house, at least a half hour walk, or she could bum a ride from someone in Pritchett's Deli.

The thought brought back memories. How many times had she and her then best friend Lucy Aimes bummed rides after a night out with some of the local girls? And a night out in Hill Top meant hanging around the old man's pub, much to the dismay of her aunt.

She pushed the memory back into the file where she kept the things she'd rather forget and grabbed her cup of tea. She stepped out of the car and balanced her tea on the hood. Pushing the front seat forward of her '69 Volkswagen Beetle - the real deal as opposed to those new remade models she would tell people, she pulled out her carry on. She'd almost tossed her belongings in a duffel bag, then last minute decided against it.

The handle of her carry on snapped in place as she pulled it out as far as she could. She thanked her guardian angel for the little inner nudge that guided her toward the carry on. If she had to hoof it, at least she wouldn't have to carry a bulky duffel bag. She could pull the carry on along while she sipped her tea. And the cool October morning wasn't too cool for a long walk. By the time it warmed up she'd be at Aunt Ruby's house.

The bump-bump-bump of her carry on as it hit the brick sidewalk on Main Street filled her ears as she made her way out of the business district. As she passed each of the mom and pop shops, she marveled at how little change had come to Hill Top. After living in New York City for the last seven years it was almost like culture shock. New York City was ever changing, a city that was a character in itself, alive and flowing with new things to see almost daily, it seemed to her. Still she was grateful for the array of worn and faded mismatched awnings that shaded her from what promised to be a day of strong, constant sun.

Determined to make the walk to her aunt's as quickly as possible, she hesitated in front of Aimes Ice Cream Shoppe. An image of herself and Lucy Aimes flashed before her eyes. She shielded her eyes from the sun with her right hand as she stood in front of the glass plate window. Her eyes scanned the familiar shop - the small aluminum tables with two vinyl upholstered chairs each, the ice cream counter, and the familiar posters and plaques on the walls. Anywhere else one would have thought the owner was going for a retro look. In truth, the shop was exactly the same as it had been when it first opened its doors in the late forties. *If I had a dime for every cone I ate here...* Being home was already affecting her. She was thinking like Aunt Ruby. Tacy shook her shoulder length brown hair and gave her carry on a sharp tug.

She took the brick walk two steps at a time, eager to escape going down memory lane any more. As she remembered, she passed the last store, Dunley's Mini Mart. For just a second, she thought about stopping in and picking up a few things for Aunt Ruby, something she'd done almost every day for her aunt when she'd lived in Hill Top. But after five years away, she couldn't even think of what to buy. Did her aunt still like Parkway margarine on her morning toast? Did she still drink the one percent milk she'd raised Tacy on?

Tacy couldn't help the smile as she remembered the first time she'd tasted whole milk at Lucy Aimes' house. She'd been shocked at the taste difference. She'd asked her aunt why they didn't have whole milk, to which her aunt had told her that 'a lady doesn't need all that extra fat'. Considering her trim frame and the fact that she didn't have to exercise every day like her girlfriends to stay that way, she couldn't help but wonder if her aunt had it right all along.

Pressing her face against the cool glass door, she stared at the store, the familiar displays at the end of the aisles touting oak tag signs with SALE in bright red marker. It wasn't even nine o'clock, too early for the mini mart to be open. She'd have to come back to town to pick up her car anyway. She could bring a list from her aunt then and kill two birds with one stone, as they say.

She was at the end of the road. Literally. The brick sidewalk of Main Street ended abruptly at the corner of Dunley's Mini Mart. With her toe, she poked at the chipped handful of bricks that signaled the end of the walk way. She stepped down onto the dry dusty ground and stared ahead of her. As a teen she'd never even thought about it.

Now she felt overwhelmed by a view devoid of stores and houses; there was nothing except trees. Her heart sped up. Maybe she should rethink her decision to walk. It wasn't too late to turn around and head back to Pritchett's and bum a ride.

The sudden heat of the sun overhead tingled at her back. She slipped the elastic band from her wrist and wrapped it around a sloppy pony tail. She could do this. She was a New Yorker. Walking was what New Yorkers did best. And plenty of it. This was no different than walking to all the auditions she'd walked to over the last several years. She'd put lots of mileage on her feet this year especially. No audition was too little. Not when it meant a chance to pay the rent without having to scramble between three part time jobs and an occasional loan from a friend. No, she wasn't turning around. She had this.

She slipped off the hoodie she was wearing and tied it around her waist. The t-shirt was a welcome relief. Grateful she hadn't chosen today to break in a new pair of high top sneakers, she started walking. The worn out black low tops she'd thrown on were already grimy. This dusty road was no match for them.

Hill Top was at its most glorious in the fall. October was an ideal month. Tacy admired what seemed like miles of trees, and yet it seemed like each one was a bit different. The range of color was stunning, from scarlet red to a burnt orange to a bright yellow, there was a little bit of it all.

She found herself feeling grateful that developers hadn't found their way to Hill Top. Acres of wooded area lay undisturbed. It was a nature lover's playground. One could wind their way through the trees and clearings to enjoy the sounds and sights of nature. As a child, Tacy had frequented these woods, lying quietly behind a tree hoping to spot a chipmunk or a deer.

Of course, there was that one time when something had spotted her. She was sure she'd felt it closing in on her, heard the sniffing sound as the hairs on her arm stood up. She'd whirled around only to be sprayed at full force by one frightened skunk. A little too late, her uncle had told her you never startle a skunk. It seemed like weeks before the daily tomato baths had kicked in, removing the last of the wretched scent from her hair and skin. "That's a lesson I'll never forget" she said aloud. No answer.

The quiet was as disturbing as the twenty-four/seven racket outside her apartment window that she thought she'd never get used to. Like the tomato baths, it had taken time. Now she barely noticed it.

But today the silence smothered her. She almost wished for a furry critter to run out at her. Anything to break up the monotony. As if the universe heard her, the rumble of a truck filled her ears. She stopped and turned around to see a frog-green pickup truck sidling up to her.

"Can I give you a lift?" A dark haired man with

full beard and mustache stared at her from behind the wheel. He was wearing a flannel shirt, the sleeve rolled up on his arm, which was perched on the steering wheel as he waited for her to answer.

"Uh, no thanks. I don't accept rides from strangers." Continuing to walk, she kept the truck in sight out of the corner of her eye.

"I'm no stranger. I live here." He was trying to keep his eyes on the road and yell out the passenger window at the same time. The pickup swerved ever so slightly.

"You're a stranger to me." As her feet picked up pace, her heart did the same. What if this guy was some kind of serial killer? What if he decided to jump out of the truck and grab her, slapping his hand over her mouth? Who on earth would hear or see them? She shuddered despite the growing heat of the October sun.

"Well, I know everyone around these parts and I know you. I've seen your picture." The truck stopped.

Tacy stood frozen to the ground, her heart beating wildly as she scanned her surroundings. Nowhere to run, nowhere to hide. Not a house in sight. She turned and faced him, trying to give him her coldest, toughest look possible.

"What picture are you talking about?" She made sure to keep eye contact with him, not missing the twinkle of laughter in his eyes. Serial killer. No, maniacal stalker hiding in Hill Top. And would she be his first victim or just one of a string of forgotten girls?

"Tacy Clark, I've been in and out of your Aunt Ruby's house so many times I lost count. I've seen pictures of you as a little girl, a teenager with braces and with your cap and gown when you graduated Hill

Top High. Get in the truck." He leaned across the seat and pushed open the passenger door.

Tacy braced herself. She was a New Yorker. She'd heard stories like this countless times, shrugging them off in a way that becomes second nature when the constant barrage of tragedy on the news desensitizes one. She decided to play her wild card. She reached into the small hand bag strapped across her shoulder.

"I'm giving you fair warning. I'm licensed to carry and I'm not afraid to shoot. And I've got good aim. Your choice." She clutched the bag tight so he couldn't see how hard she was shaking. She would have kicked herself if she could have. Why, oh, why didn't she take Annie's advice and gotten a small hand gun? She almost laughed. All this time she and Annie had thought city life warranted protection and here she was in Hill Top, a town with 496 people to be exact, and she wasn't here more than two hours and she was being accosted.

The hairy top lip and chin broke open to reveal surprisingly white teeth making for a pretty nice smile. Too friendly a smile for a maniacal stalker, she thought.

"Would you like me to call your Aunt Ruby so you can check with her about me?" He shook his cell phone at her and then tapped a few buttons.

Tacy stood rooted to the ground. It seemed to her she had no choice anyway. It's not like she could run off while he was making his phone call. With a quick glance, all she saw were more trees.

He was holding the phone out to her, the passenger door still gaping open. He shook it and gave her an exasperated look.

"Ok, I'll put her on speaker. But I don't know if

you'll hear your aunt's voice from all the way over there. You can come a little closer. I don't bite."

Tacy inched closer to the truck but far enough that she figured his hands couldn't reach her, just in case. She strained her ears to listen. There was no mistaking Aunt Ruby's voice. She stepped close enough to grab the cell phone from the could-be serial killer's hand and took it.

"Aunt Ruby? Is that really you?" She was listening so intently to the voice, she could hear her ears ring.

"Tacy, is that you? Brody tells me he found you walking the street alone with a suitcase. What on earth is going on?"

~

Brody Porter eyed Tacy Clark out of the corner of his eye as he drove along the dirt road. She didn't trust anyone. He could tell. He knew the type. He knew a lot about types of women. He'd had to learn about them the hard way, but he was all the wiser now. He couldn't blame her. There were few people he trusted himself these days. Ruby Clark was one of them. The woman had a heart of gold. If it hadn't been for Ruby he would have packed up Cami and everything they owned and headed out of Hill Top a year ago. He counted his blessings every day and having a neighbor like Ruby Clark was the greatest of all. Still, he was good at 'typing' women and his gut said spoiled. Tacy Clark looked like a spoiled brat. What else could you think about a young woman who hadn't come back to visit the woman who had raised her in over four years? He noted the shoulder length brown hair which she had sprung from a band and promptly slipped on her wrist.

He ran his eyes over her once, noting the slender figure and modest curves in the right places. He'd even gotten a whiff of her perfume, some kind of exotic plant or spice he didn't recognize. A city girl. Of course Ruby had told him that. He knew she was a musician with some orchestra or something. He knew Ruby had raised her best she could after Tacy's mother had been killed in a car wreck, out joyriding and having fun as she tended to do.

"So, what else do you know about me?"

She was staring right at him, a look of skepticism in her eyes still, even after the poor old woman had gone back and forth on his phone, convincing her that he was ok. Imagine her thinking he was some kind of lunatic or something. This was Hill Top. The only lunatic they had here was Larry the deer, who had taken to destroying some of the outside displays the shop keepers kept outside at night.

"I know you're a musician. I know you left home seven years ago and you haven't been back since your Uncle Jerry died four years ago." He was looking her in the eye, having stopped to let a family of ducks cross the road, on their way to Gatts Lake no doubt. Her brown eyes darkened, matching the dark blue jeans she was wearing. He watched her shuffle in her seat.

"I was home for the funeral. I just couldn't stay long. I had auditions I had to be back in the city for."

Tight lips and a head facing forward told him the conversation was closed. That's all right. He wasn't interested in hearing what she had to say anyway. Her life was of no interest to him. He had only one interest now and that was getting her to Ruby's house safe and sound. Crazy girl. Who in their right mind would walk a half hour in this heat? He could ask her that.

"What happened to your car?" He saw her shoulders drop.

"I don't know. I stopped at Pritchett's for a cup of tea. I came out and got in and when I went to start it, she wouldn't catch. Nothing. She's dead. I know she's old but she was running fine up until today."

"She?"

She turned to him. He thought he caught a quick grin.

"Yes, she. Her name's Becca. She's a nineteen sixty-nine Volkswagen beetle."

"Do you name all your cars?" He couldn't help laugh. He wished he hadn't.

"I've only owned two for your information and yes. So I'm taking it you don't have a name for this...this noisy thing."

He chewed his lip and thought about it. When he was young, back in his twenties, he'd had a car with a name. It was an old sports car and she'd name it Speedy, she being his at the time girlfriend. He tightened his grip on the steering wheel. Carrie Ann, his estranged wife, hated his truck. He could see already he wasn't off the mark with this woman either.

"No, I don't. I'm a grown man. I've got better things to think about than naming a truck." He put his focus back on the road, grateful that Ruby's was only a minute down the road. Let her deal with Tacy, the poor woman. Maybe that's why she didn't ask her niece to come back to the orchards to help. Maybe the girl was more trouble than she was worth. He signaled to turn right into the long tree lined drive that led to Ruby Clark's farmhouse. He heard Tacy suck in her breath.

For just a minute, he wondered if he'd made a mistake emailing Tacy Clark to come home. Then he pulled himself together. No. He'd done the right thing. All he had to do now was deal with two women who had no idea what he'd done to bring them together. In her late sixties to mid-seventies and recuperating from a broken hip, he was pretty sure he could handle Ruby. But judging from the fight Tacy Clark had put up about getting into his truck, he had a feeling he had a fight on his hands. And he was finished with fighting with a woman.

## Chapter Two

As the pickup rolled up to Aunt Ruby's farmhouse, Tacy took it all in. She'd expected the house to be a ramshackle mess, the lack of Uncle Jerry's care taking evident by peeling paint, broken porch rails and overgrown bushes and grass. Her mouth gaped as she scanned the meticulous lawn and expertly shaped bushes. The clean bright white of the house said it had been recently painted. She stepped out of the truck and dropped her carry on to the ground with a thud. The familiar sight of the stone steps matching the base of the house were like an old friend. She'd spent countless hours perched on them in the sun, reading a book or practicing violin. She studied the rails, noticing not only that not a one was broken, but that they, too, had been painted fairly recently.

"Is this all you brought? Or did you leave some stuff behind in your car?" He was standing only inches behind her.

She pulled herself away from her walk down memory lane and turned to him. "No. That's all I brought. I figured I won't need much for the short time I'll be here." She saw his eyes darken, his lips tighten.

"Fine then. I'll bring this inside for you. Ruby's probably in her room resting." He cut around her rather brusquely, her carry on suspended in air from his right hand.

She followed after him, wondering why Ruby would be in bed so late in the morning. For as far back as she could remember, both her aunt and uncle were up at the crack of dawn. It was almost ten in the morning. Lying in bed this late could only mean one thing - something was wrong with Aunt Ruby.

The screen door banged shut behind her as she stepped inside. The first thing she remembered was how sunny Aunt Ruby and Uncle Jerry's living room was. The bright October sun flooded the big room, the brightness accentuating the worn spots on the floral upholstered sofa and love seat. Nothing had changed in the room. The dark wood coffee and end tables still held the white doilies her aunt was famous for gracing over surfaces. The angel statues her aunt loved so much, the ones she'd not been allowed to touch until she was a young teen, stood frozen in time on each end table.

Her heart fluttered as her eyes landed on the frame hanging above the sofa. Her eyes skipped the cousins, aunts and uncles, zeroing in on the one person's face she hadn't looked at in four years - her mother, Fern. It never ceased to amaze her how little she resembled her mother. The willowy long haired blond with light blue eyes was polar opposite to Tacy's plain brown eyes and dark brown hair. There were no pictures of her father to add the missing pieces to the puzzle.

"Coming?" Brody Porter, as he formally introduced himself back in the truck, stood waiting, her carry on having been set in the hall outside her old bedroom.

His impatient, arrogant attitude was irritating her as much as the fact that he knew which room was hers. Imitating his earlier action, she pushed past him without a word and stepped into her aunt's bedroom.

Ruby Clark sat upright, propped up against a trio of pillows, her bedspread tucked around her. From the look on her face, Tacy knew in an instant that she was not expecting her visit.

"Tacy! My goodness I didn't know you were coming! Why didn't you call?" Aunt Ruby pulled herself up as the bedspread fell away. Tacy couldn't help but stare at her frail aunt, a woman who used to climb ladders during harvest season and could wield a hand lawn mower with ease.

Instinctively, she went to her aunt and wrapped her arms around her, feeling the change in her once robust body. She breathed in the familiar scent of rosewater.

"I didn't call because..." She stopped talking and turned to Brody Porter, whose arrogant frown now was replaced with a sheepish look. The email. She should have known. Aunt Ruby didn't email her. Aunt Ruby didn't even own a laptop or a smart phone. Brody Porter sent the email and he put her aunt's name on it.

"You did it. You sent the email, didn't you? And you signed my aunt's name on it. You didn't tell her, did you?"

His brown eyes met hers, a flicker of amber caught the light coming in from the window next to Ruby's bed.

He fingered his beard, obviously thinking before he chose to speak. He stepped in and stood at the foot of Aunt Ruby's bed.

Tacy wondered if her aunt had paled from shock or if she was just very sick and no one had let her know.

"I did. I sent you that email because I knew Ruby wouldn't do it herself. I know she doesn't have a computer, and she could have called, but I knew she wouldn't. She's too proud to ask for help. I did it because she needs you and she won't say so herself."

Tacy could almost feel the tension in his rigid body.

"Don't you think that's a bit nervy?" She wanted to have a snappy comeback. She wanted to jolt him the way he'd jolted her with his calling her aunt from the truck. Instead her words made her sound mousy and she was tired of people seeing her as the mousy, quiet type.

"Honestly, I don't. I did it with the best of intentions. Ruby needs help. Harvest season is coming and those apples need to be picked. And she's only got one man. I can help here and there, but she needs someone who knows the orchards. She needs you to bring in more help and get those apples harvested. The annual harvest festival is in a little over a week. It was an emergency situation and I did what I thought was best."

Tacy knew the type. The type who thinks he's got to make everything right. The guy who likes to play superhero. The kind of guy who likes to be the boss and tell everybody else what to do. Well she didn't answer to anyone and certainly not a complete stranger. Glancing at her aunt, she wondered if this neighbor of hers wasn't too involved in her aunt's business. She'd have to put that right. Hopefully, she could do it in a week's time because that was all she had. In one week she expected to be back in New York City auditioning for Upper West Side Orchestra, a fairly new music ensemble that was quickly becoming esteemed in the music world. It was the best opportunity she'd had in years and she didn't intend to miss it. Not for anything.

She felt a niggle of guilt. Would she ever stop feeling guilty for not being here for her aunt when Uncle Jerry was ill? She pushed away the inner debate she'd had hundreds of times and focused on her aunt.

"Aunt Ruby, what's happened? Are you sick?" The pounding of her heart spoke over her aunt's whisper like voice.

"No, Tacy, no. Nothing like that. It's not what you're thinking. I had a little spill..."

A gruff voice spoke over both her aunt's meek voice and her thumping heart.

"It was a fall, Ruby. She fell and broke her hip. She had surgery and never even told you. She's home recovering now, but she could use some help around here."

Tacy ignored him even as the words stung. "Aunt Ruby, why didn't you call me? A broken hip is serious. I would have come home." As she said the words, she felt the old niggle of guilt again.

She'd let Aunt Ruby down once before. She'd been so consumed with her music career she hadn't come home to give her a hand when her uncle was sick. By the time she cleared a week to come, she ended up coming home for his funeral instead. That was four years ago and she still couldn't live it down. At least not to herself.

"Tacy, I was fine. Hill Top Hospital took good care of me and I spent a week in rehab. Just because I'm lying in this bed does not mean I'm in bad shape. I was just about getting ready to get up when Brody called me. When he said he found you walking along the roadside, well, I'll be honest and tell you it gave me a scare. I couldn't imagine what happened to you, especially since you hadn't called to say you were coming. I didn't want to bother you dear. I may be getting older, but I remembered that you had something important coming up."

She was shaking her head, the short silver bob the only hairstyle Tacy could ever remember her aunt having.

A framed picture of Tacy and her mother rested on the night table. Her mother's smiling face beamed at her, as if she were watching from above, even though Tacy couldn't say she'd ever felt her mother's presence. Maybe because she'd been so young when her mother had been killed in that car accident. She wanted to tell her aunt that she was important too. That what happened to her mattered to Tacy. She wanted to, but the words wouldn't come.

She'd been raised in a good home with her aunt and uncle. They'd treated her like their own, sparing her from going to a foster home. Yet, she had such a hard time expressing her feelings to them. She'd never said 'I love you' to either her aunt or uncle. It was easier to not love anyone. She'd lost her mother and then a year ago, she'd lost the man she'd finally allowed herself to love. She looked away from the past she barely remembered and took her aunt's hand.

"I would have come, Aunt Ruby. Of course I would have come to help you." She thought she heard a slight snicker coming from Brody Porter's lips. Not wanting to upset her aunt, she chose to ignore it.

17

"Oh, dear. I don't want to keep you away from your music. I'm fine. I'm on the mend."

Out of the corner of her eye, she saw Brody's hand go up.

"The harvest, Ruby. What about the harvest? The church is counting on it. I don't mind looking in on you here and helping around the house, but you need help out in the orchards. You've got to get those apples picked and ready for the festival."

Tacy sat down at the foot of Aunt Ruby's bed, ignoring him. For now.

"I'm here so you've got my help. Let's take it one step at a time and see how you're doing, okay? And I really wish you had called me. I would have come. I swear." Ruby waved a thin pale hand at her.

"I know you would. You're a good girl, Tacy. Now you two go on and get out of here. I'm going to get myself dressed and get this day started."

Tacy watched Brody head out of the room. As her aunt swung her legs over the side of the bed, she leaned over and kissed her cheek.

"If you need any help you holler." She got up and headed for the door. She watched her aunt shuffle to the closet and closed the door behind her.

Brody Porter wasn't in the hall like she'd expected he would be. She headed down the hallway and looked around the living room. She doubted he'd just left. She walked into the kitchen and spotted him standing at the sink, a cup of coffee in his hand. About to walk right up behind him and get down to business, she stopped. There in the corner behind the kitchen table was her old violin case.

Seeing the old battered case stirred up

memories. She could still remember the day Uncle Jerry had brought that violin home for her. The normally gruff and tough man was beaming, pleased with his find. One of the men who had been working the orchards that day had the violin for over twenty years. A hand injury had abruptly stopped his playing and it had lain in the back of his closet for years, until the day Uncle Jerry had told him that 'little Tacy' wants to play the violin. The brown case blurred before her eyes. Refusing to let this arrogant neighbor, friend – or whatever – of her aunt's see her cry, she ripped the hoodie from her waist and swiped her eyes. His back still to her, she waited until she felt composed enough before approaching him.

"Who are you exactly?"

In no rush, he turned around and eyed her.

"I told you before. I live next door. The old Hastings house. I bought it two years ago. I've been a friend of your aunt's since. She's been a good friend to us as well."

Us?

"Oh, so your wife knows my aunt as well?" There was no reason her heart should flop like it did. She had no interest in this arrogant, bossy neighbor of her aunt's.

"No, by us I mean my daughter and me. Your aunt has helped me in a pinch many times. She's been a good neighbor to me and I've tried to be a good neighbor back."

The mention of a daughter threw her. She'd planned to give him a peace of her mind. Let him know just how wrong he'd been to sneak around behind her aunt's back, sending an email without her knowledge.

There was no mention of a Mrs. Porter. It sounded like it was just him and his daughter.

"Okay. I just don't think it was right for you to send an email without my aunt's consent. And you didn't even mention what was wrong. If you could find my email to get me to come here, why didn't you email me when she first fell? Why didn't you let me know she got hurt?"

"I was going to, but your aunt forbid it. At the time she was in the hospital getting taken care of, so I figured there was no harm. Then she spent a week in rehab. They only let her come home because I said I'd be here to take care of her. The trouble is I can't take care of Ruby, run my shop, take care of my daughter, and organize the harvest for the annual festival. I could use an extra pair of hands."

Tacy rearranged her words in her mind. Somehow she'd lost her steam. She watched him walk to the doorway, peering down the hall for Ruby.

"I could understand that. I just don't like being tricked like that."

~

He had been right. She was a spoiled bratty woman and she was a spitfire to match. He'd felt her anger the minute she'd set foot in the kitchen. He had no doubt she was ready to give him a lecture. Being tricked. He certainly knew a thing or two about that. He couldn't blame her. He might have gone about things all wrong, but it was all for Ruby.

*And I need that harvest of apples.*

He felt guilty thinking it, but it was true. He was concerned about that harvest. The trees in that orchard were about to burst with ripe apples. What a waste it would be not to get them picked in time to sell at the annual harvest festival as Ruby had done for so many years before. He'd seen it the first year he'd been there, when Cami was just about a year old. He knew how the town counted on the proceeds from the apple sales to fund the upcoming year at the church preschool. He'd helped out with the guys working the orchards for the sake of offering an extra set of hands.

Little did he know that only two years later, he'd be depending on that harvest to fund the preschool his own daughter needed every day. Without the preschool he'd be in trouble. His new coffee shop, Brews & Bites, was struggling already. If he didn't put in more time to expand his hours and offerings, he could very well be forced to shut down. Without the coffee shop he would have no way to provide for Cami. The last thing he wanted was to fail her the way her mother had. He shook the image of Carrie Ann Porter, Carrie Ann Ryan, her stage name, now, out of his thoughts.

"Okay, fine. I apologize for *tricking* you to get you here. But your aunt told me you had something big going on, being a career girl and all." He couldn't stop the sneer as the words *career girl* gritted out from his lips.

"I know. I heard that. But I would have come. Maybe I can't stay very long, but I would have come."

She was standing by the sink now, a cup of coffee in her hand, the trembling ever so slight.

"Yes, you would have come. So let's just go from there because there isn't that much time. I need...your aunt needs you to hire the help to work the orchards so that the harvest doesn't go to waste. I'd be glad to still give a hand around here with the house or

21

the apples, but can you take care of that?"

He saw the skeptical look in her eyes. He could see she wasn't stupid. No doubt she was questioning his interest about the orchards. Women were so much smarter than men gave them credit for. He knew that now.

She put the cup of coffee down and stared him in the eyes. Still he thought he saw her top lip quiver.

"Okay. I'll take a look at the notebook that my Uncle Jerry kept about the harvest and see who I can round up. I don't even know who worked here last so it may not be that easy. I'll get started. But don't worry. You won't have to do anything around the house. I'll see to my aunt's business from here on in."

She was giving him his walking papers. Trouble was, he had something at stake here. And no bossy spoiled niece of Ruby's was going to screw up something so important to his daughter. For now he would give her a chance to get started. But he had every intention of staying as close to Ruby as he had been for the last two years. Whether Tacy Clark liked it or not.

# Chapter Three

Tacy set a plate of scrambled eggs and a cup of hot black tea in front of her aunt. She placed a napkin with a fork and knife next to it. She wasn't the greatest of cooks, but she felt good. She was taking care of Aunt Ruby, and that's all that mattered.

"Oh, Tacy, dear, I can still cook." Aunt Ruby's walker was parked against the wall, the violin case beside it. Tacy had helped her aunt get settled in her seat, feeling her unsteadiness against her arm.

"I'm sure you can. You were always the best cook around. But I want to cook for you for a change. I can't promise they'll be anywhere near as good as yours." Tacy watched her aunt dig in, dipping a forkful of egg in the neat circle of ketchup she'd poured for her.

"This is delicious. I'm afraid I'll get spoiled between Brody's cooking and you being here taking care of me. I'll have no reason to get on my feet as soon as possible."

Tacy smiled as she dropped the frying pan and utensils she'd used to cook into the hot soapy water in the sink. She wiped her hands on the lemon yellow terry cloth dish towel hanging from the refrigerator handle and patted her aunt's small shoulder.

"You take your time and eat. I'm going to pull out Uncle Jerry's notebooks from the desk and take a look at things. I'll get started getting the guys together for apple picking. I'm hoping since tomorrow is Saturday they can jump on in." She walked out of the kitchen and turned right into the living room. Trying hard not to look at all the picture frames that seemed to fill every corner of the room, she cut through an opening to the small windowless alcove where Uncle Jerry's office was.

The small alcove off the living room had been the perfect spot for an office. It only accommodated the barest essentials - a desk and chair, bookshelf and floor lamp. Tacy's eyes darted from frame to frame, forgetting about all the pictures her uncle had hung on the walls. One picture in particular was of his own parents standing under an apple tree back when they'd owned and worked the orchards, more than fifty years ago.

Tacy had known since she was a child that the orchards had been passed down for generations but she'd never met her uncle's parents. For that matter, she'd never met Aunt Ruby's parents, her mother's parents. There were pictures of them in Ruby's room, but in here the pictures told the story of the orchards.

Her eyes stopped on the picture of herself crouched on the lowest branch of an apple tree, an impish look in her eyes. She couldn't have been more than five years old. She remembered that t-shirt she was wearing in the picture, the smiling monkey face on the front with a curly tail running up the right shoulder. Most of all she remembered her Uncle Jerry hoisting her up on to that branch and letting her play Tarzan.

Next to that frame was a picture of Uncle Jerry perched on the very same branch, making a goofy face for the camera. He'd always been about fun and games; he'd always been about Tacy. It wasn't Uncle Jerry who'd whispered those words all those years ago that she wasn't supposed to hear. Little did her aunt know she'd been outside their bedroom door, about to knock when she'd heard her aunt say them. The picture of Uncle Jerry blurred. Tacy swiped at her eyes and shook herself. *Toughen up, Tacy.*

A whoosh of dusty air brushed her face as she pulled up the front of the mahogany roll top desk. The three spiral notebooks she remembered her uncle writing in stood in the last slot as if frozen in time. Envelopes, papers and index cards filled the other assorted slots in the desk. She pulled open one of the four drawers on the right hand side where he'd kept pens and pencils. Everything was in its place. With quick deft moves she opened the other seven drawers, taking a quick look and closing it just as quick. It looked as if Aunt Ruby hadn't touched anything since her uncle had passed. She sat down on the antique bankers chair that her uncle had scooped up when the bank had been remodeled and grabbed the familiar red notebook she'd seen him thumb through countless times.

Unlike Aunt Ruby's meticulous penmanship, Uncle Jerry's reflected his personality. Large loopy letters and chicken scratch, as her aunt had called it, filled the pages of the notebook. Even still, Tacy found the list of pickers with no problem. Next to each man or woman's name was a phone number. Elias Hatcher had only an address with two stars next to it. She scanned the page, flipping it over to the other side to see if he'd made note of the meaning of the two stars. There were none. For now, she'd start calling everyone on the list and see what she could do. She pulled her cell phone out of her jeans pocket and checked the time. It was almost noon on a Friday. She supposed it was as good a time as any other. She ran a finger over the receiver of the old rotary phone that perched at the edge of the desk. It was the only phone in the house.

She punched in Thomas Everly's number into her cell phone and waited for the ring. A recorded voice startled her. The number had been disconnected with no forwarding number given. She picked up a pencil from the drawer and ran a line through Thomas Everly's name.

"I'm afraid you're going to get quite a few of those, dear."

Tacy turned in her seat. She hadn't even heard her aunt come into the alcove. Her aunt was standing in the opening, her arms holding tight to her walker. Tacy watched as she maneuvered the walker with wheels so she could roll into the little room.

"What do you mean?" She put her cell phone down and got up. Her aunt gestured for her to sit back down. She was managing fine.

"I'm afraid Thomas Everly passed away a year after your uncle did. Several of those pickers were older than your uncle himself. I'm wondering if you'll be able to get any of them."

Tacy chewed the end of the pencil as she stared at the names on her uncle's list.

"Well, I'll give it a try. Don't even worry. If I can't get enough this way I'll get them another way." She was about to punch in the next number when she stopped.

"Aunt Ruby, do you know why this man's name has no number? All he has next to him are two stars."

Her aunt leaned over the notebook and squinted.

"I'll take a look, but my glasses are in the kitchen." She took the notebook from the desk and held it close to her face, than pulled it further back.

"Oh, that chicken scratch of your uncle's," she smiled. "I can see the name's Elias Hatcher. Those two stars were your uncle's way of noting first picks. Elias Hatcher was a hard working picker." She nodded, pleased she had solved the small mystery.

"Yes, but why isn't there a phone number to call him?" Tacy tapped the man's name with the pencil's eraser.

"Oh, yes. Elias Hatcher was a stubborn old man. He was older than dirt then and he refused to come into the times. He didn't have a phone. Your uncle used to make the ride up to his place to tell him when he needed him."

Tacy thought about it. The last thing she had planned on was picking up any men to work the orchards. Besides that, she wouldn't have a car until she could figure out what was wrong with hers. She had to get it back to the farm to do that first. An image of Brody Porter's frog green pick up flashed in her mind. *Nope, I'm not asking him for any help.*

"Well, maybe for now I'll leave him for the bottom of the list. I'll work on getting these other men lined up. This way I can see how many other pickers I'll need to round up in case they aren't available."

She felt the light touch of her aunt's hand on her shoulder.

"You do whatever you think is best, Tacy.

You're taking on a huge task and I appreciate it. But we have to face the fact that we may not be able to pull it off this year."

Tacy watched her aunt maneuver her walker towards the entry way.

"But how did you do the last two years or so since Uncle Jerry passed?"

Ruby stopped moving. With her back to Tacy, her words came out like a whisper.

"I didn't. We didn't pick them in time for the annual fall harvest festival those years."

Tacy stood up and wrapped an arm around her aunt, helping her back into the living room.

"I don't understand. Brody Porter made it sound like the orchards were harvested last year for the festival. He sounds like he's very concerned about making sure the apples get to the festival this year. He emailed me specifically about the harvest and how important it was to get those apples picked in time."

Aunt Ruby looked winded, as if the effort to get from the kitchen to the alcove and back to the living room had been too much for her. Or maybe it was all this talk about the orchards.

"Well, it is important for him this year. You know the proceeds from the harvest during the festival go to the church preschool. Without that money the church preschool won't be able to continue to operate."

"How does a church preschool have anything to do with Brody Porter?" As soon as the words came out of her mouth she knew she'd answered her own question. He'd mentioned a daughter.

"This is the first year little Cami is eligible for the preschool program. He wants to make sure the preschool stays open. He needs the preschool so he doesn't have to worry about Cami's care while he's at work."

It all made sense to her now. Like pieces falling into place in a puzzle, she understood the urgency of the email. This wasn't about Aunt Ruby. This was about Brody Porter wanting something for himself.

"What about the little girl's mother?" Her heart pounded so hard she worried her aunt could hear it in the quiet of the large living room.

Ruby made a tsk tsk sound and fiddled with the necklace around her neck. That's when Tacy noticed the string of painted macaroni noodles.

"She doesn't have a mother. Or at least not anymore. Cami's mother left her and Brody when she was an infant. He doesn't say anything about her but that much I know. The subject is closed, poor man."

*More likely poor woman,* she thought. From his attitude back on the road when he'd found her, she could tell he was a bossy man to deal with. Still, she wondered what kind of woman would leave her baby behind. Leaving her husband was one thing, but a child? She thought of her own mother and how she'd died when she was a toddler. She was only three years old and she barely remembered her.

"How old is this...Cami?" Her body stiffened as she waited for an answer.

"She's four years old."

Tacy didn't miss the way her aunt's cheeks beamed as she said it.

"That's tough." Tacy meant it. It was tough. She knew. Four year olds need a mother. Girls need a mother period, she thought with a pang. She tried to push the image of a cherubic toddler from her mind. She didn't have time to get involved with Cami Porter. She only had a week and she needed to get down to business.

"If you'd like to recline here on the sofa, I'll get you whatever you need. You can relax while I make those calls. What can I get you?"

Tacy spotted the petite wooden stool with the embroidered upholstered top she'd loved to sit on as a small child. She picked it up from the corner it was tucked in and slipped it in front of her aunt. Aunt Ruby placed both feet on it and smiled.

"Now, you don't have to spoil me like this. I'm expecting to be mending quick and getting back up and round."

"I'm sure you will, but in the meantime I'm here and I want to take care of you. Shall I get you a book?" Tacy scanned the built in bookshelves that covered the wall between the oversized picture window and the wall where the sofa was. Her aunt had always been an avid reader. As her aunt's eyes drifted towards the books, Tacy studied her sitting there on the sofa. Her aunt had worn her prematurely gray hair in that short pixie style for as long as she could remember. But the fleshy cheeks and bright blue eyes she'd remembered were gone, replaced by noticeably thinner cheeks and lackluster eyes. She supposed after Uncle Jerry's passing, her aunt hadn't been the same.

"You know what I think? I think I'd like to sit out on the porch on my rocker with my knitting. It's not too hot today, is it?"

Tacy thought about the October sun, the early morning heat beginning to beat on her back. These would be the last few warms days of the fall in Hill Top. Cooler weather was days away. The cool crisp air of apple picking season had been one of her favorite times on the farm. She thought of that picture of herself as a small child perched on the branch of that apple tree.

"No, it's beautiful today. I think it's a great idea for you to enjoy the warm air before it changes. I'll get your knitting and set you up outside."

Tacy shot down the hallway and opened the door to her Aunt's bedroom. That's when it hit her. This wasn't the spacious bedroom of her aunt and uncle that she'd remembered. This in fact was her mother's old bedroom. After her mother's death, her aunt had kept the room exactly as her mother had had it. Tacy had had her own room next door.

Tacy made a note to ask her aunt why she'd moved out of the bedroom she'd shared with her uncle. For now she had to find her aunt's knitting basket. Trying hard to avoid any painful reminders of her mother, she glanced around the room. Spotting the wicker knitting basket in the corner beside the dresser, she scooped it up and left the room.

"Let's get you settled out there first, and then I'll bring everything out to you after." She dropped the basket by the front door and walked over to her aunt with the walker in her hand. With a gentle touch, she helped her aunt up from the sofa and put the walker in front of her. She ran ahead of her to open the front door. Brody Porter had left the big wooden door open. A gentle breeze had been blowing in through the screen door all morning. Tacy pushed the screen door open as wide as it would go and waited for her aunt to make her way out to the porch. She was grateful the shiny new walker had small wheels that let her aunt glide across the porch as opposed to the metal walkers one had to lift with each step. She could see her aunt wouldn't be able to handle one like that. She let go of the screen door to help her aunt get into the white painted rocker.

"Now this is lovely."

The cheerful words were a good attempt to cover a wince Tacy could hear. Aunt Ruby gripped the arms of the rocker and closed her eyes.

"Aunt Ruby, are you ok? Shall I get your knitting now?" Tacy felt herself go cold, despite the warm October sun flooding the wooden porch. Her aunt's eyes fluttered open.

"Yes, I'd love that. And then I'll stop being a bother and you can get to work."

Tacy darted back in to the hallway and grabbed the knitting basket she had placed by the front door. She dropped it on the floor next to the rocker her aunt was sitting in.

"You are no bother. What shall I grab out of here for you?" Tacy poked a hand around the basket. The touch of the soft yarn balls at her fingertips felt comforting, reminding her of a time long ago when her aunt would make her hold her hands very still while she wrapped yarn around them.

"Do you see that pink project wrapped up in there? I'd like to get back to work on that. I'm making Cami a scarf for the winter."

Tacy held the pink yarn bundle in her hands for a moment, noting the soft fleecy material with intermittent splashes of turquoise running through it. She stared at what she thought was an odd choice for a complimentary color. As if her aunt could read her mind, she laughed out loud.

"Cami picked the yarn out herself. I had her with me the day I went shopping in Big Mart. That shade of blue matches her coat perfectly."

Tacy thought Cami sounded quite smart for a four year old. It wouldn't surprise her one bit if she were precocious too, considering that father of hers. An image of Brody Porter came to mind. Dark haired with sideburns, mustache and a full beard; the man was full of hair. He did keep himself groomed from what she could tell, but she wondered what his face looked like. And how old he was. He seemed older than her twenty five years for sure, especially with a four year old daughter. No matter. Brody Porter was no concern of hers.

"That's great. Well, I'm going to head inside and get the rest of those calls made. We'll need to see where we stand with the pickers before we can do anything. Do you need anything else?" She waited for her aunt to answer, but Ruby's eyes were on the front walkway leading to the porch.

Tacy turned to see Brody Porter heading up the walkway. And running a few steps ahead of him was a little girl, her golden hair catching the wind as she hurried for the steps. Noisy sneakered feet bounded up the wooden steps then came to a halt when she saw Tacy standing there.

"Who are you?" Small hands clutched the sides of her peach colored sun dress, bright blue sneakered feet slightly turned inward. The side part in her shoulder length hair was mussed, strands falling wayward in all directions.

Before Tacy could answer, Brody Porter's shadow cast across the porch, suppressing the sun from herself and her aunt.

"Cami insisted on coming to see you today, Miss Ruby. I hope you don't mind. I can easily take her to work with me since it's not a school day today."

Tacy bit her lip. She knew what he was doing. What nerve the man had. He'd gotten her to leave her music, come home to run the harvest and now he was fishing for free child care from her invalid aunt. The little girl was now standing alongside her aunt's rocker, her small hands twisting the pink yarn of her scarf. She watched as her aunt finger combed the little girl's mussy hair. What could she say? The last thing she wanted to do was cause a row and upset her aunt. And it would be just what Brody Porter expected, since she could tell he already thought she was selfish and didn't want to help her aunt out.

"Oh, no, leave her here with Aunt Ruby and me. I'm going to be inside working but I'll keep an eye out on them both." She whipped on her brightest, sweetest smile. And she didn't miss the smirk on Brody's lips.

"Well, then, I'll be going." He ignored Tacy and looked right at her aunt. "Ruby, you have the coffee shop's number on the refrigerator should you need me."

As he started down the porch steps, Tacy called out as loud as she could so he'd be sure to hear her.

"That's okay. We won't need you at all." She glanced at Aunt Ruby, who was deep in chatter with Cami. It looked like she had more than one job on her hands right now - taking care of Aunt Ruby and getting the message across to Brody Porter. His help wasn't needed around here anymore. As the screen door closed behind her, she tried to ignore the thought nagging at her. *But what happens when it's time to head back to the city?*

the end.

## Chapter Four

Brody pushed open the door of Brews & Bites coffee shop and hurried to the counter. Normally he always opened on Fridays and stayed at the shop the entire day. Today, however, his routine had been interrupted. He'd opened the shop at six this morning and then passed the torch at eight to Lucy Aimes-Hurley, his most trusted employee. Though he'd been hesitant to hire the twenty-seven year old, just his own personal issue, he'd been desperate enough to give her a try.

And he'd been pleasantly surprised. The young woman had proven herself as hardworking and reliable more than once. Not only had she came early, stayed late, perfected every drink the shop offered, but she'd saved his neck several times by picking Cami up. She'd even taken Cami to her own house for several weekends. Cami had taken a shine to Lucy and her husband Jake, but it was Scoops, Lucy's beagle, that had become the talk of their home. Brody was already fending off questions of 'when can we get a dog?' and 'can we get a dog like Scoops?'

Lucy's head was dangling inside the glass cabinet as she wiped the inside glass clean. She popped up, spotted Brody and gave a wave, her auburn hair braided to one side falling to her back.

"Hey, Lucy. How are things going here?" He

walked around behind the counter and looked around. She didn't disappoint. Everything was fairly orderly considering she'd handled the morning rush all by herself. Hopefully in a month or so, when the preschool could fit Cami in both classes, he would be able to hire another counter person. Another set of hands could keep the tables wiped down, the dishes clean and refill whatever they ran out of as the two of them handled the morning rush. And the back room where the ovens were could use another set of eyes. Right now he only offered pastries, but his goal was to eventually bring in artisan sandwiches that he would make back there along with some homemade soups. He had several recipes of his grandmother's he was eager to add to the menu.

"I have to say we really are getting busier in the mornings. This morning I had all I could do to keep up by myself. It was quite the balancing act, but you'll be happy to know I pulled it off." A freckle covered hand gave his shoulder a gentle punch.

"You're a lifesaver. It's after one. Why don't you take off? I'm going to need you here tomorrow all day." Brody started clearing away the glass pitchers they used to create the fancy coffees he had brought to Hill Top. He set them carefully into one of the two sinks behind the counter and turned on the hot water, shaking a bottle of powdered soap into the water. He could soak them during the slow time. The next rush of business would be the after work crowd around five or so, those who were looking to grab a cup of coffee on their way home. And because it was Friday they would get the high school kids and the twenty somethings who were looking to hang out and plan their night out. In Hill Top, a night out consisted either of a movie, of which the local theater only offered two choices, hanging around the small local park, or fishing at Gatts Lake.

"Ok, I think I will." Lucy untied the beige apron from her waist, rolling it up in a ball. "How's my sweet Cami doing?"

He turned to answer her and watch her back as she disappeared into the back room. She was back in seconds, a rolled up apron sticking out of her over-sized hand bag.

"She's good. She's spending the afternoon with Miss Ruby." He grabbed his own apron and tied it around his waist. Standing in front of the register, he keyed in his code and the drawer flew open. He scanned the morning's take and closed it with a snap.

"I'll bet that little girl is like a healing balm for her. I believe Ruby's hip will be mending that much faster with Cami around."

"Well, maybe so, but she's not the only one that's around." After he said it, he regretted it.

He knew that Lucy and Tacy had been best friends while growing up. He also knew that Tacy had left town without even saying goodbye to Lucy. She was staring at him with a blank look.

"I'm sorry. I'm not sure how you're going to feel about this, but you might as well know now. I'd feel terrible if you found out from someone else."

"Spit it out, Porter. What are you talking about?" Hands on her hips, she was frowning now.

"Tacy Clark is back in town. She's come home to take care of her aunt for a little while." He saw her bright green eyes darken, the frown deepen. She began fishing in her bag for here keys.

"Well, I don't feel anything about that. It's none

of my business what Tacy Clark does. It's her aunt, so I'm glad for Ruby. She deserves the help. Lord knows she didn't do a thing when her uncle was ailing."

Brody only nodded his head. He'd heard the stories from the ladies in town. The seniors from the center Ruby was friends with had pretty much acted the same way. His own family was fractured. His father had left when he was a child and his mother had passed when he was in his twenties. His mother's mother had blamed his father for his mother's death in her late forties. At best, he had a strained relationship with his grandmother and when she was sick she'd made it clear to his aunt, his mother's sister, that she didn't want his help. He knew what it was like to be on the outs with family. But it irked him that Tacy had the opportunity to come to her aunt's aid and she hadn't bothered. At forty, he wished he had some family left for Cami to spend time with. Tacy didn't know how lucky she was. It bothered him that Tacy took that sweet aunt for granted. *It doesn't matter what she does. Just let her get the harvest underway.* He shouldn't feel guilty for what he did. He did it for Ruby.

"Can you open with me tomorrow? Now with the harvest season in full swing I think we'll catch a lot of people coming up to apple pick looking for coffee and something to eat on their way."

The change of subject seemed to calm her down. He hadn't missed the flush of color in her face when she'd talked about Tacy Clark coming to her aunt's.

"Sure thing. Are you sure you're going to be able to make it in that early? What are you planning to do with Cami?" She stood in front of the door, her hand on the metal handle about to push it open.

Brody thought about it for a moment. In the past, he'd dropped Cami over at Ruby's since the woman was an early riser. That was another thing that prompted him to email Tacy. The woman was sleeping in later than he'd ever remembered. He was worried about her. Maybe the combination of losing her husband and the broken hip were making her depressed. He thought about what Lucy said about Cami being a healing balm to the woman.

"I was thinking of bringing her in with me, but it is kind of early. She's such a sleepy head too. I'll see if I can arrange for her to make an early visit to Ruby..." He was going to add 'if that's okay with Tacy' but thought twice. He'd seen already how the name had upset Lucy. There was no need to bring her up again. He'd only wanted to give her a heads up so she wasn't caught off guard should she run into Tacy one day in town. It was the least he could do. He liked Lucy. He wasn't sure he could say the same for Tacy.

"I'm sure Ruby would like that." Lucy gave a wave and walked out the door.

Brody rolled up his sleeves. Might as well get to work on all the dirty cups and pitchers Lucy had used this morning. He grabbed the organic sponge he'd just ordered a carton of and dunked it into the soapy water. He scrubbed each item one at a time, rinsing the soapy water from them and lying it on the towel on the counter next to the sink to air dry.

After the sink was emptied, he stepped into the back room. The ovens he used to bake pastries were all cold to the touch. Most baking was done in the wee hours of the morning, in time for customers to enjoy them fresh. Get here early enough and you just might get something straight out of the oven. To get a jump on things, he decided to set up the trays with cinnamon rolls so they'd be ready to go straight into the oven first thing in the morning. He also had a new croissant, dark chocolate, he was eager to try with his customers.

With a quick wash of his hands, he opened the refrigerator and pulled out a huge container of dough he'd made earlier today. He dropped it on the steel work table and reached into the glass jar of flour. Dumping the dough onto the table, he began kneading the dough. It was one of the things he enjoyed most about his job. Kneading dough was a great way to smooth out your frustrations. He was thinking about Cami. He just had to get her into the dual class program. It was the only way he could see himself expanding the shop and making enough money for them to survive. He also was thinking of doing a music night one night a week in the coffee shop. He was thinking that a Friday night of music would be a big hit with the younger people looking for something to do. Staying open late on a Friday might bring in just enough to justify being closed on Sundays. He would have preferred to be open on Sundays but the old blue law from years ago was alive and well in Hill Top. With the exception of Evie's Cafe and Aimes Ice Cream Shop, the business district in town was closed for business on Sundays.

"Anybody back there?"

The gruff voice startled him out of his reverie. He dropped the clump of dough in his hands and swiped them down his apron. He hurried for the front counter. The last thing he wanted was to have a customer complaining about service.

A man in a dark gray suit stood at the counter, his hands resting on the glass as his head swiveled around slowly, taking in his surroundings. A pair of designer sunglasses rested on the top of his head. Brody felt the man's eyes appraise him as their eyes met.

"What can I get you?" The guy made him uncomfortably conscious of the flour coated apron he was wearing. Still, he kept it on and met his stare head on.

"Sure. I'd like a large cup of Brody's Afternoon Power Punch." He was pointing to one of the three blackboards that hung from the wall behind the counter.

"You got it." Brody zipped around behind the counter, grabbing a jar of organic beans that he had to order from Seattle to make his own special coffee mix. A lot of the college kids ordered the power punch to pull all-nighters, especially during finals week. One of the secrets of his special coffee was the fact that he only ground the beans at the time of the order. As the grinder whirred to life, he tapped the keys of the register. If he'd opened the shop in Chicago he could have easily gotten five dollars for a cup of his special mix coffee. But this was Hill Top and the people who ordered this were mostly high school and college kids - kids with a limited budget. So he settled on four dollars, and so far he hadn't gotten any complaints.

"Four dollars." Judging from the way this guy handed him a twenty he could tell he was used to paying for what he wanted. He counted out the change.

"I haven't seen you here before. On your way to the orchards for apple picking season?" Nobody dressed like that for apple picking, but he had to get the conversation started somehow.

His face was expressionless. He barely shook his head.

"I don't pick apples." He took the money Brody handed him and slipped it in the inside pocket of his suit jacket.

The conversation was over. Brody poured the ground beans into his newest machine and slipped a to-go cup under the spout. Figuring the man had nothing to say to him, he kept his back to him and waited.

"I would like some directions though."

Brody turned around and faced him. The guy had strolled over to the counter where they kept sugar, honey, milk and other coffee accompaniments. He walked back to the counter and gave Brody what seemed like a forced smile.

"Where do you need directions to?" Brody didn't like the guy. Whether it was the smile or what, he didn't know. He just got a weird feeling about him. He only wished he'd gotten that weird feeling, that whisper of intuition, when he'd married Carrie Ann.

"I'm looking for Elias Hatcher's home. I was hoping you might be able to tell me how to get there."

Brody knew where Elias Hatcher lived. He'd only talked to the man two or three times. Everyone in town knew Elias was a hermit. The first time he'd talked to Elias was the day he'd moved in to the house next door to Ruby. The man had been out on the porch talking to the woman. He'd spotted Brody and Cami and promptly run off. Ruby had said nothing about the man. The second time he'd seen him was only a month or so ago, after Ruby had returned home from the hospital. He'd stopped by with a bag of vegetables, from his garden Brody had assumed. Brody had been at

Ruby's that day and so he'd taken the bag from the man and promised to let Ruby know he'd been by. Just as quickly as he'd come, he had hurried off. He'd asked Ruby about the man only to find out he'd been a picker for the family orchards every year until Jerry Clark had passed away.

Brody tossed around the idea of saying he didn't know where the man lived. The guy hadn't offered his name or why he was looking for him. He thought about the old man who lived alone in the ramshackle house he'd driven by one time. This was a service oriented business and giving customers what they asked for was part of that service. He was still new to town and if he wanted to expand and succeed he needed to give people what they wanted.

"Sure. If you take Main Street all the way north to its furthest point, you'll see the sidewalk ends and it becomes a dirt road. There's nothing much after that point except land and a scattering of houses. Just continue straight on that road until you pass the Clark Orchards. You'll see the sign. About five miles past the Orchards you'll see a woodsy area with a sign at the entrance of the drive that says keep out. Take that drive to the end until you see a big old farmhouse. That's Hatcher's place."

"Sounds simple enough. Thanks." Coffee in hand, the guy headed for the door. Without a wave or word, he stepped out into the afternoon sun.

Brody watched him as he stood out in front of the shop looking around. Then he was gone, presumably on his way to Elias Hatcher's place. Maybe the guy was a relative coming to see Elias, he thought.

Before he could convince himself of that, the

door opened and a trio of teenagers came in. The Pritchett boy, the Dunley girl, and Mary Ellen West were familiar faces. They'd been the very first customers he'd served the day he'd opened his door.

"How's it going guys?" He started getting their lattes ready.

They ordered the same thing every Friday. As the trio settled in at the corner table they occupied every Friday afternoon, he grabbed a white chocolate brownie with dark chocolate chips, cutting it in three pieces. He carried the plate over to the table.

"You guys feeling like being my guinea pigs today?"

He put the plate in the center of the table and backed out of the way. Three eager hands swiped the chunks of brownie. He watched them shove the chunks in their mouths, mumbling 'yum' and 'whoa'.

"I'm going to take that as a yes." He laughed and walked back to the counter.

He reached for the heavy porcelain mugs he used for customers having their coffee in and lined them up across the counter. He filled a jug with milk and began to stretch the milk, gently getting the air into the milk. He kept his eye on the milk until the foam was perfect. He began to spin the milk. He thumped the milk.

Satisfied it was perfect, he began to pour it, when he heard the door open. He looked up and saw Tacy Clark heading for the counter, her eyes on him. What on earth was she doing here? He loaded a small round tray with the three lattes on it and whisked it over to the trio's table. Deep in conversation, they didn't notice him. He met Tacy in the middle of the shop.

"I didn't expect to see you here." He folded his arms across his chest, as if stopping her from going any further. The idea that she might come into the shop had never crossed his mind. He watched her peer past him, her eyes taking in the counter, scanning the menus hanging on the wall behind it.

"I didn't even know this place existed. It sure wasn't here when I left."

"Is there something you want?" She was a city girl. She probably wouldn't last without a latte or whatever fancy coffee she drank. It didn't surprise him.

"Actually, I wanted to talk to you."

She must have seen the look of concern in his eyes.

"Oh, Cami is fine. It's about the pickers. I'm running into a bit of a problem."

He bit his lip to keep from smiling. She wanted to talk to him. He'd heard her say she wouldn't need him at all. She sure changed her tune quicker than a pair of shoes. He pointed to the table at his side and pulled out a chair. Surprisingly, she took it with a grateful nod. He took the one across from her, a safe distance between them.

"Okay, tell me what the problem is."

As he listened to her talk, he tried to ignore the way the sun caught the flecks of amber in her brown eyes. A small scar just below her left eyebrow twitched. He'd noticed she'd changed into jeans and a navy blue t-shirt, making her look more relaxed, despite the tell-tale twitch.

*Don't even think about it. The only thing you should be thinking about is getting that harvest picked.*

"So, my aunt says you have a way with the high

school kids around here and that's why I thought maybe you could help. I didn't want to ask, but I don't have that much time. I was hoping I could get this organized and be on my way."

She reminded him of a balloon that someone had untied, the air rushing out of her and then she was motionless. She was sitting there opposite him, spent. She was waiting for him to talk. Talking wasn't his strong point. He was a doer. He got things done. He glanced over at the trio of regulars who had polished off his brownie and were now alternating between sipping and laughing.

"I might be able to get a few of the teens that come in here. I'd have to talk to them."

"That's just it. Aunt Ruby says you speak their language."

Brody laughed out loud. Yes, if their language was lattes and iced coffees then he spoke their language.

"Ok. I'll start checking around and see what I can do." Brody stood up and tucked his chair in. When the tables were empty he liked the way the place looked with all the tables tucked in tight. He waited for her to stand but she remained seated.

"Is that the only problem you needed to talk to me about?" He felt the hairs in his beard twitch.

He'd come to take that as his gut talking to him. He watched her face redden as she stood up. He hadn't realized how tiny a woman she was. It made him want to protect her, why he didn't know. The last time he'd followed his *knight in shining armor* instinct, he'd ended up with Carrie Ann, an actress who was too young for him and looking for a place to stay until she landed on her acting feet again.

"I need someone to help me tow my car back to Aunt Ruby's house." She blurted the words out, her hand tucking and untucking hair behind her left ear.

He was going to have to learn how to put his feet down. When was he going to learn to put a limit on helping other people? Specifically female people. One problem per customer per day. Only thing was, Tacy wasn't a customer. She was his neighbor's niece and she was too close for comfort.

# Chapter Five

His facial hair didn't hide the way he'd clenched his teeth when she'd asked him for help getting her car back to Aunt Ruby's. She hadn't missed the look on his face. She'd been just as thrilled about asking him for help. It was the last thing she wanted to do, but she had no choice. If Orley's Garage had been open, she would have paid to have the car towed to her aunt's. She'd dialed the number of the garage that had been tacked up on her aunt's refrigerator for as long as she could remember and was surprised to hear the recording that the number was no longer in service.

Her aunt told her that Orley had decided to close up shop and move to a warmer climate after battling with arthritis for more than twenty years. Not only did she not have a way to get the car back to her aunt's house, she also didn't have a way to get it repaired. No doubt she'd have to go to the next town over, Warwick, to find a garage that could repair her car. With only a week or so visit, she was beginning to feel overwhelmed with her growing to-do list.

As she stood on the curb watching Brody poking under the hood of her beetle, she glanced at her phone in her hand. It was close to five o'clock. She'd forgotten to look in Ruby's freezer to see what she had to cook. Tacy was planning on making something for her to eat, and she remembered her aunt and uncle's habit of eating early suppers.

"I don't think you're going to be able to do anything under there." She didn't mean to sound impatient, but she didn't have all day. Who was she kidding? The day was almost over. It was October and the days had grown shorter. At most, they had maybe an hour and a half before sunset.

He jerked his head up from under the hood and stared at her. "How do you know what I'm capable of doing?"

The semi-grin on his lips suggested he was having a little fun at her expense.

Tacy shifted herself from side to side, feeling a flush of heat spread from her neck to the top of her head. She wasn't going to let him get her goat, as her aunt would say.

"Well, if you're going to be awhile, I'm going to run into Dunley's and pick up something for supper. Aunt Ruby likes to eat by five thirty, and it's already five o'clock."

He snapped the hood shut and walked over to where she was. He stood in the asphalt road directly in front of her. Being elevated by a few inches didn't mask the fact that the man had at least eight inches on her.

"Are you hungry?" His eyes locked on hers.

The sun might have been slowly making its descent, but intense heat enveloped Tacy. She stepped backward to get some distance from him, afraid to breathe on him.

"I'm talking about Aunt Ruby. She's probably starving by now." She ignored the rumbling of her own stomach.

"An hour or so isn't going to make a difference. Let's go grab some dinner."

He swiped his hands on his jeans and jumped up on the curb, standing too close beside her. Tacy couldn't remember the last time someone had made her so uncomfortable. *Get yourself together. He's just some coffee making dad.*

"Aunt Ruby is probably waiting for me to make her supper. And I'm sure you need to pick up Cami and get her taken care of as well." She grabbed the opportunity to break away from him and jumped off the curb, heading for the front of the Beetle, where its trunk was. She feigned deep absorption in the car's trunk as he hovered behind her.

"Actually, I called her before we got here. I had left a cold salad in the fridge for her last night. I figured she'd be hungry, so she and Cami are going to eat dinner together."

Tacy laid her violin case back down in the trunk and turned around. He stood with his arms folded, waiting for her to say something.

Her tongue felt too big for her mouth. She wished she had thought to grab a cold drink before they walked over to Pritchett's Deli where her car had been stranded.

"Oh, well, I guess that takes care of them, but I really don't want to leave Aunt Ruby alone. I have a lot of things I need to do for her." To her own ears she sounded like she was fumbling. She opened her mouth to add more, when she felt his arm brush against her waist. He pulled her to him.

"Look, let me take you to dinner. I brought you here so let me do this as a way of thanking you for helping out with the harvest."

Tacy unwrapped herself from his grasp and inched towards her car.

"That's not necessary. I told you I want to help my aunt. If I had known sooner that she'd broken her hip, I would have come then. You don't need to buy me dinner. I really don't have time to get...to spend with anyone other than my aunt."

She saw him stiffen, one arm dropped to his side while he tucked his left hand into his jean pocket.

"Don't make it more than it is." He pushed past her and made his way to the back of the car. With more force than needed, he threw open the hood. He bent over the engine.

Tacy studied his thick dark brown hair. That wasn't what she'd meant. She replayed her words in her head to convince herself of what she'd meant. She'd said it wrong. She knew what she meant to say, but it hadn't come out quite the way she'd intended. He was so arrogant, and yet, she was feeling apologetic. She knew it was because of the little girl, Cami. She ambled over to him, hesitated for a moment, and then tapped his right shoulder.

"That didn't come out the way I intended. I'm sorry." As she waited for him to respond, the rumbling of her empty stomach broke the silence.

He turned around and grinned at her. She wasn't blind. The hair, the mustache and the meticulously groomed beard were attractive. The man didn't want for looks. He broke her. She flashed him a grin.

"Come on. This'll be here when we're done. We can probably still catch the Friday night special at Evie's Cafe." He offered her his arm and she took it.

They left his truck and her Beetle out front of Pritchett's Deli and started walking down Main Street, passing the familiar shops she'd passed on her way back into town.

"The Friday night special?" She liked the way he kept up with her. She had been sure he'd be a stroller, living in a small country town like Hill Top. Instead, she was surprised to find he had a city-like stride.

"Yup. It's Cami's favorite." He had a ridiculous, goofy grin on his face. She had to ask.

"Okay. You got me. What is it?"

"Hotdogs and beans." He was stifling a laugh.

His eyes teased her, dared her not to laugh.

Tacy couldn't remember the last time she'd laughed out loud over something so silly.

"That's special all right. I take it you and your daughter make the special often?"

They were standing out in front of Evie's now, staring through the storefront window where the red and white checkered cafe curtain had been pulled open. He steered her to the door and pulled it open, feigning a bow as he held it for her. She stepped inside laughing. Several diners looked up from their menus and meals to look at them. From the arch of their eyebrows, Tacy wagered a few remembered her.

She couldn't help but wonder if they remembered her as the niece that didn't come home to help when her uncle was sick. Everyone in town had loved Jerry Clark. Starting to feel uncomfortable, she looked away and focused her attention on her dinner date. No, not her dinner date. He was her aunt's neighbor and he was just trying to do a good deed.

She'd let him. There was no harm in that.

A gum-cracking ponytailed hostess in a white t-shirt and denim skirt skated over to them. She ran an eye up and down Tacy and dismissed her. She turned to Brody Porter and gave him a big smile.

"Hi, Mr. Porter. Where's Cami tonight?"

Brody was beaming with pride. It was obvious he loved his little girl.

"She's having her supper with Miss Ruby tonight. Winnie, this is Tacy Clark, Miss Ruby's niece. She's come from New York City to take care of Ruby and help out with the annual harvest festival."

The girl gave Tacy a second once over, her head tilted to one side. She cracked her gum loudly and gave Tacy a half grin. She couldn't have been more than seventeen years old. At twenty-five, Tacy looked at her as a kid. Tacy stared back at her, mainly trying to place the girl's face. She'd probably been about ten years old when Tacy had left Hill Top. She'd babysat a few of the local kids, but this girl wasn't familiar at all. The name Winnie wasn't ringing any bells.

"Nice to meet ya." She grabbed two menus and signaled for them to follow her. She dropped the menus on the table of a booth at the back of the cafe.

Brody waited for Tacy to be seated before sliding on to the bench opposite her. A customer waved to Winnie, who promptly hurried off.

Tacy watched Brody study the menu as he sipped from the glass of water that was brought to their table.

"Do we even need menus?" She smiled as he looked up from the menu.

"If hotdogs and beans suit you, then I guess we

don't. I don't want to twist your arm. You're free to order as you please."

His smile seemed forced to Tacy. All she'd did was crack a joke about not needing menus. She was beginning to see why maybe Brody Porter was on his own with his little girl. Still, the image of the little girl niggled at her. *Little girls need a mother.* The thought popped up again. She ignored it and attempted to make another stab at conversation with him.

"No menu needed. I'm going to take Cami's recommendation and go with the hotdog and beans. And an iced tea. I love brewed iced tea."

She was going to ask if he offered iced tea in his shop but stopped. Better to see where this was going first. He flashed her a genuine smile.

"You can't go wrong. Kids tell it like it is. And if you're an iced tea lover you'll have to come by the shop one day and try mine. I've got a secret recipe you might like."

"I'll do that. I was even thinking of getting Aunt Ruby out. I'm going to call her doctor first and get the okay, but I think it would do her good. Maybe we'll both stop by and check that tea out together." He seemed pleased with her answer.

Winnie was at the table now, pad in hand, and waiting for them to notice her.

"Winnie, we're both going to have the Friday special. Two orders of the hotdog and beans plate. And Tacy would like an iced tea."

Winnie was scratching slowly at her pad, her eyes on Brody as he spoke. She glanced at Tacy with little interest.

"Will that be all then?"

Tacy gave her a smile and nodded. Brody gave her a wave. The gum cracking teen sauntered off.

With their orders taken, they sat there in silence. Tacy studied the cafe, noting that like most everything else in Hill Top nothing had changed. The familiar booths with wooden benches and dark wood tables were exactly as she remembered. The handful of tables in the center of the cafe were matching wood, the only difference being the chairs had red and white checked upholstered seats. The old-fashioned soda shop Tiffany-style lamps hanging over each booth looked as dusty as they had when she'd been a child. At the side wall of the cafe was probably the only counter fountain left these days. Heavy, old clunky metal machines that cranked out delicious drinks, like egg creams and real thick shakes, whirred away as the counter girl darted from diner to diner, taking orders and putting down plates filled with homemade fries. She looked back at Brody to find he'd probably been studying her as in depth as she'd been studying the cafe.

"So. How do you like running a coffee shop?" She figured it would be a safe enough subject to explore with the man. That and, obviously, his little girl.

As she suspected, he perked up, a grin on his face and she was sure she saw a glint in his eyes.

"I love it. It's a great lifestyle change from what I used to do."

"Really? What did you do before starting the coffee shop?" He had her interest.

She loved learning about people. It never failed to interest her hearing about what people did or where they used to live before she met them. As a musician, she didn't get to talk to too many people. Playing in the pit was a discipline. There was no time for chatting and mingling. It was almost an unspoken understanding among her colleagues. After performances, most everyone packed up and off they went. When she wasn't performing, she was practicing alone in her apartment. If she didn't get this next audition, she'd be practicing in a parking lot somewhere, because she wasn't going to be able to come up with her rent much longer. New York City was such a rock and a hard place. On one hand it was the land of opportunity and some of the best paying ones at that. On the other hand, it was also one of the most expensive places to live. You might be able to land a good paying gig, but if you didn't, you couldn't afford to live in the land of opportunity for too long.

"I was a financial advisor." He stopped talking and picked up his glass of water.

"In Hill Top?" She stared at him. He put his glass down and laughed.

"No, nothing like that here for sure. In Chicago, where Cami and I lived before we moved here. I've only been in Hill Top a little over two years."

"Chicago. Wow. So, you left a big city, and what I'm guessing was a prominent job, to come start a business in Hill Top? Did you always want to be a barista?"

"Actually, yes. It's something I'd been toying with for some time. But I didn't come here just to start a business. I came here because I wanted to raise my daughter in a small town. I visited here ten years ago. It was actually the weekend of the harvest festival. I was passing through on the way to help a buddy fix up his new place about fifty miles from here. I saw the signs for the festival and decided to take a break from driving and check it out. So when I was looking for a new place to…uh… start over I guess...I thought of Hill Top. I bought the house next door to your aunt sight unseen, with the exception of a few pictures on the internet."

Tacy's eyes widened.

"Sight unseen? That's taking quite a chance. What happens if you don't like what you've bought? It's too late then."

"Might be. But in this case I liked it. The Hastings house needed a lot of work, but that's right up my alley. And the yard is great for Cami. She loves dogs, so we might even get a dog down the road."

Tacy's heart leaped. That was one thing she'd never had. She'd always wanted a dog, but Uncle Jerry had been allergic to them. He'd just about given her everything else but a dog. She'd had chickens, pigs and even a wounded deer that they'd nursed back to health. Funny. Up until this moment, she'd actually forgotten all about that deer. Or those wonderful pets Uncle Jerry had given her.

"Every kid should have a pet. It teaches you responsibility. And they're great company. At least I know a dog would be."

Brody's eyebrows went up.

"So, you're a dog owner?"

She shook her head, brown wisps falling in her eyes. She pushed them out of her eyes.

"No, not in the city. My apartment is way too small for a dog. I barely have enough room for myself to move around in. But if I had room I would get a dog."

"Well, there's plenty of room at Ruby's for a

dog." He watched her as she picked up the iced tea Winnie had brought her.

"I don't think Ruby is in shape to take care of a dog. And I'm only going to be here for a week or so. Ten days at most. I'll have to put a dog on my ten year list."

About to bite into his hotdog, Brody's ears honed in on her words.

"Ten year list?" He was staring intently at her.

"Yes. You know, like a goal list, or a sort of bucket list, but with things you want to do or accomplish within ten years. I'll have to add a dog to mine."

He was grinning from ear to ear at her now. The hotdog he'd picked up was back on his plate. Instead, he picked up the bottle of mustard and coated his hot dog. She could feel it coming. Without even looking at her, she knew what he was going to say.

"So, what else is on that ten year list of yours? If you don't mind my asking."

Tacy clenched her hot dog and bit in. She actually did mind. She hadn't shared the details of her ten year list with anyone. She only had one or two friends in the city. They'd managed to set her up on blind dates that would have been better off never happening. There wasn't anyone she could share the details with. That was one thing she missed. Having a best friend to share those kinds of things with.

"Oh, it's just some silly things I want to do someday. I'd rather not."

A tender look came over him. She saw it in his eyes, in the way he reached across the table and patted her hand. At the first tingle, she pulled her hand away, pretending to need to pick up her iced tea. As if he suddenly remembered something, his eyes darkened.

"Some things are better left unsaid."

The look on his face cooled her faster than the iced tea in her hand.

But she'd seen the look in his eyes when he spoke about Cami. Nothing cool there. She almost envied little Cami. Uncle Jerry had tried his best to be the father to her that she'd never had. Still, there was that empty spot in her heart. She wondered what Brody Porter would be like. Not as a father, but as a husband.

Feeling the heat rise, she clung to her iced tea, gulping it to the point that she was sure other diners could hear her. But it wasn't thoughts of Brody Porter that stopped her mid sip. As her eyes tried to look away from Brody, she caught a familiar face standing alongside the cafe counter. Lucy Aimes, her one time best friend, hadn't changed a bit.

## Chapter Six

"Is your hotdog okay?"

She heard the words, but she was in a fog. Lucy Aimes was making her way past the tables and booths, heading straight for the back of the cafe, to their booth.

"Uh, yes, of course." Tacy took a halfhearted bite of her hotdog, barely tasting it.

She stared at the beans on her plate, but it was no use. Lucy Aimes was standing in front of their booth now. To her surprise, Brody slipped out of the booth and bear hugged her. As they hugged, Tacy gave her long lost best friend a once over, noting that she still wore her rust colored hair in the side braid she'd sported most of her life. Brody released her and the two women were left with no choice but to face each other.

"Tacy Clark, you haven't changed one bit. Although I see you've cut a few inches off your hair. I like the shoulder length look on you."

Though the words sounded like two friends having a casual chat, Tacy could see Lucy felt as awkward as she did.

"Yes, it was just too much work having it long like that. It's a lot easier this length. You look good." She meant it. She looked good. What's more, she looked happy. She wanted to ask how Lucy knew Brody but he took care of that himself.

"Lucy works part time for me. When she's not working for me she...." Brody stopped talking.

Tacy's eyes darted from Brody to Lucy. She hadn't missed the look Lucy had given him, silencing whatever he had been about to say next.

"Oh, that's nice. How are your parents?" It was the obligatory question, what her aunt would have expected her to say. You always asked about family members when you ran into old friends. She saw Lucy's face light up.

"They're great. They still work the ice cream shop everyday even though they have a few dependable workers that would free them up."

Tacy remembered Lucy's older sister. Theirs had been a rocky relationship, with Lucy always feeling she had to compete with Cory. Cory was the honor student, the girl who got a track scholarship, and the girl who got the perfect guy, something she nor Tacy had been able to do. A glint of light from the hanging light overhead sparkled from the rings on Lucy's hand. It appeared Lucy had finally gotten her guy. Lucy's eye caught hers as she stared at the sparkling rings. She held up her hand. "It's Lucy Aimes-Hurley now."

"And your sister, Cory? How's she doing?" She saw Lucy's eyes cloud up and for a moment wondered if something had happened to Cory.

"Oh, she's great. She's got two little boys and we just found out she's expecting a girl soon." The deflated look in her eyes belied the happy words.

"Wow. That's wonderful. Well, send her my congratulations." Tacy had always been on Lucy's side when it came to her sibling. As an only child, she hadn't really been able to understand what went on between the two sisters, but she could sympathize. Cory had been the apple of their father's eye, something Tacy had never known.

"Sure, I will. So how long will you be in town for?" Lucy steered the conversation away from her sister.

"I don't have too long. Maybe a little over a week. I have an audition that I have to be back in the city for."

Out of the corner of her eye, Tacy saw Brody shuffle in his seat. Lucy nodded her head in understanding. Brody said nothing.

"Well, good luck with that. I have to run. I put an order in at the counter for Jake, my husband. He loves the thin sliced corn beef sandwiches here." She chuckled and turned her attention on Brody.

"So, I'll see you at six tomorrow for opening, right?"

"Absolutely. I expect we'll have a busy morning now that people are heading up here for the picking season."

"You work with Brody?" Tacy couldn't help herself. The burst of words surprised her two companions as much as it surprised herself.

Brody gave her a steely eyed look, as if she'd done something wrong.

"That's right. I don't know what I'd do without Lucy. It's not easy finding loyal people you can depend on."

Even though she knew he was talking about the coffee shop, Tacy couldn't shake the feeling he was talking about something more and he was directing it at her.

"Thanks, Brody. Enjoy your food." Lucy turned to go and then stopped. Tacy stared at the back of her head, the familiar lines of her braid slightly crooked, fine hairs creeping out from their restraint. She turned around and looked at Tacy.

"I hope you and your aunt have a good visit, Tacy." With that she headed for the counter, her bulky tan boots clunking against the cafe floor.

Tacy picked her hotdog back up and tried to dig in. She'd barely eaten half of it, her stomach still felt empty but the growling somehow silenced. She put the hotdog down and picked up a French fry, swirling it aimlessly in the little puddle of ketchup on her plate. She let the French fry linger in the ketchup and looked up at Brody, who was popping the last bit of hotdog into his mouth.

"How come you didn't tell me that Lucy Aimes works for you?" She struggled to get the words out from a tongue that felt dry and parched, regardless of how much tea she'd sipped earlier.

He looked her square in the eye. "I just did. Besides, I didn't think I needed to tell you who my employees were." He kept his eyes on her, steady without a blink.

"You sure felt the need to tell me that I needed to come home."

"Because that's your business, not mine. The coffee shop has nothing to do with you. Aunt Ruby's orchards do."

"That's pretty hypocritical when I happen to know that the orchards do have something to do with you." She saw him flinch ever so slightly. She wanted to cinch the conversation.

"I know you're only interested in getting the orchards picked for the harvest festival because your daughter needs the church preschool to remain open." She waited.

"Yes, that's true. But I also care about Ruby and I don't think it's right that you don't stay in touch with her. You take care of family. That's the right thing to do."

"Well, since you know so much about my relationship with Ruby, I'm sure you know all about Lucy and I. You could have told me she worked for you. That's all." Her words sounded feeble and foolish in her own ears.

Brody was signaling for Winnie. The gum cracking waitress stood in front of them, her right hip jutting out impatiently.

"Winnie, I'll take the check." Brody held out his hand as Winnie ripped a page from her pad.

She dropped it in his palm, gave Tacy a quick look and sashayed off.

Tacy picked up the small bag she'd brought along with her. Her hand found her wallet and she snapped it open, pulling out a ten dollar bill.

"This is for my half." She dropped the ten dollar bill in front of his plate. His eyes narrowed at the bill, his lips in a tight line.

"I said this was my treat. You can put that back in your wallet." He tucked a twenty and the bill under the ketchup bottle and slid out of the booth.

Seeing a few heads had turned their way, Tacy swiped the ten dollar bill from the table and tucked it in her jeans pocket. Irritated, she followed him through the cafe and out the door into the cool evening air.

"Let's see about getting that car of yours back to Ruby's house. I've got a few things to do and I've got to get Cami." Looking stiff, he took exaggerated long steps down Main Street back to Pritchett's Deli where Tacy's car waited.

Tacy did her best to keep up in silence. The air between them felt charged. Too annoyed to talk, she decided to hold her tongue. She still needed his help if she wanted to get her car back to Ruby's. Once she got it there she wouldn't need to deal with him anymore.

Then she remembered she'd asked him to round up some pickers for the orchards. It seemed like every time she tried to distance herself from this man, she found herself two steps back right alongside him.

~

The woman was getting on his every last nerve. She was acting as if he'd wronged her. He had no obligation to let her know who was working for him. Like a pesky fly, guilt fluttered at the back of his mind. Why did he feel slightly guilty? Yes, he'd taken it upon himself to send her an email asking her to come home and help her aunt. She had some nerve accusing him of an ulterior motive. The guilt had sprouted wings, fluttering wildly. As if he could brush it away, he swiped at his brow.

He stood over the engine of Tacy Clark's Volkswagen Beetle, hoping he could at least get it up and running for the short ride to Ruby's house. The sooner he got it and its owner home, the sooner he could be free of them.

The conversation he'd had with Tacy about finding pickers loomed in his mind. Yes, there was that. If it weren't for Cami, he would have washed his hands of helping her in any way. Instead, tomorrow he'd talk to a few of the local teens that popped in and out on Saturdays and see what he could do. He'd like to think once he got a few pickers for her he'd be done. But deep down inside he knew it wasn't true. He'd just have to limit how often he saw the woman. He thought of how much time Cami spent with Ruby. Well, that was Cami. He didn't have to stay with her and Ruby.

"What do you think?" She was leaning in from the curb where she stood, a look of caution in her eyes.

It was like she'd forgotten the incident in the cafe. Typical woman. She was obviously just concerned about getting what she wanted. It was a shame that he wanted to get the car running just as badly as she did.

"I'm going to try one more thing I just thought of. We'll see." In his mind he crossed his fingers. He poked through his pockets, hoping to find a rag from the shop that he had a habit of tucking in his pockets.

"Do you have any rags I can use?" He turned his attention to her.

Her head was bent over her cell phone, dark locks of hair having fallen across her forehead. The glow of the street light above them formed an almost halo-like light above her head. He resisted the urge to laugh. The woman was no angel. He'd seen that already.

She looked up at him, a blank look on her face. He guessed she'd been too involved in whatever she was looking at. She blinked and pushed the phone back into her pocket.

"Oh, oh sure. Let me look in the trunk. I'm sure I can find something." She ran around to the front of the car, pulling the lid open. He listened to her fish around her belongings for a moment and then slam the top shut.

With a funny look on her face, she approached him with slow steps. In her hand was a bright orange sequined clump of fabric.

"What is that?" He narrowed his eyes to get a good look at it.

The funny look turned to annoyance. "It's a blouse. I wore it when I was playing for a wedding of a friend." Her nose wrinkled as if she'd caught a distasteful scent in the air.

He bit back the urge to laugh, not wanting to invite the possibility of engaging in any fun with her.

"Fine. Throw it." The less contact the better, he thought. She tossed the glittery balled up fabric at him and he caught it. He balled it back up and leaned under the hood of the car. With the fabric secure in his hand, he swiped it up and down the wire in his other hand. Satisfied, he looked up at her to see she still looked irritated.

"What?" He snapped.

"You didn't tell me it was going to get dirty." She looked at him with wide eyes.

"Well, what did you think I was going to do with it? Go dancing?" He heard her let out an annoyed breath of air.

"Of course not. I'm not stupid. I just didn't realize you were going to ruin it." She was frowning.

"Well, do you want to get it back to Ruby's or not? Sometimes you've got to sacrifice something to get what you want." He stood directly in front of her, his eyes giving her back what she was giving him.

"Yes I do. And please don't lecture me about

sacrificing. You don't even know me."

The words came out with force, but he had a feeling that if he reached out and touched her, she'd tip over.

"Then let me do what I have to do." He left her dangling there while he went over to the driver's side. He crammed his long legs into the car and adjusted himself in the seat when he realized he didn't have the keys to start her up. He stuck a hand out the window and waved, hoping she'd be looking at him instead of that phone of hers. Within seconds she was standing outside the driver's door, a questioning look in her eyes.

"I need the key to start her up." He held out a hand, watching as she fished the key out of her back pocket. She dropped it in his hand and stepped back, almost as if she expected something to happen when he switched on the ignition.

He ignored her and focused on the car. Slipping the key into the ignition, he turned it. The engine caught and the little car roared to life. He looked over at her and saw a smile spread across her face.

"Let me drive her back to Ruby's." He tossed her his keys. "You drive my pickup truck." He saw her clutch his keys.

"But I've never driven a truck before," she protested.

He closed the door, afraid if he stepped out of the small car he may never be able to fit himself back in.

"Pretend it's a car and just drive. It's a straight ride. You'll be fine." He saw a look on her face he couldn't place. Hesitation? Fear? Was she actually afraid of something? Maybe he'd found the weak side of this self-centered woman.

He made a mental note not to let it get to him. He waved at her to get in his truck. He watched as she turned and hurried to his truck. She opened the door and pulled herself up into the cab. Within seconds his truck roared and she pulled away from the curb. He steered the tiny car away from the curb and followed behind her, keeping a safe distance in case the car should cut out suddenly.

It was dark now, a little after seven at night. The roads leading out of Hill Top weren't lit except for the moonlight and stars above. But this road, the road that he'd found on her only hours before, was a straight ride with no obstacles or sudden turns to worry about. His truck rumbled along in front of him, Tacy's dark hair tossed about from the wind of the open windows.

Brody fought the urge to rub his cramped left leg. He was thankful the ride only would take a few more minutes. The less time he had to think about Tacy Clark the better it was for them both. His eyes caught the blinking light on the back of his truck as she signaled to turn into the driveway of Hill Top Orchards. He flipped the turn signal on the Beetle and followed behind his truck.

On another night, he would have slowed his truck to admire the lush surroundings. Ruby Clark's property was nothing short of magnificent. The trees that shaded the long driveway were beginning to change color, the once dark green leaves becoming a golden light color that brightened and guided their way to the farmhouse. He imagined Tacy Clark had no time to notice how beautiful her surroundings were.

The glow of lights on the first floor of the

farmhouse always were a welcome sight. It reminded him of his grandmother's Victorian home and all the summers he'd spent running through the gardens there. For the life of him he couldn't understand why Tacy would leave Ruby and the beautiful home the woman had given her after her mother's death. Ruby had told him the story of Tacy's mother's fatal car accident. Having lost both of his parents, he felt for her. But she had a home to come home to, yet she hadn't. Not in almost five years.

He put the impossibly small car's transmission in first gear, pulled the parking break, turned off the engine, and opened the door. Untangling his legs, he stepped out onto the dirt driveway and stretched his aching back. Tacy had turned the ignition off in his truck and was heading towards him now.

"Guess she's good to go." An awkward smile met his eyes.

"Yeah, well, you got her home, but don't get too confident. You should really get her to a mechanic and see if there's something going on. You don't want to end up stranded somewhere again." He wanted to add 'and you might not be lucky enough to have someone to rescue you', but he resisted the urge.

She was nodding her head in agreement to his surprise.

"Oh, no, I plan on taking her to a garage I found in Warwick. Hopefully they can straighten out whatever's wrong before I need to get back to the city. In the meantime, I figure I can use Aunt Ruby's car to get around."

He nodded and wondered how she planned on getting the car to Warwick. It was at least a forty minute ride. What if the car broke down while she was driving there by herself? He was about to ask her just that when he stopped himself. *You've got to stop playing the knight in shining armor.* Instead he handed her back her keys, keeping his hand extended so she could give him his.

"Well, I'm sure they'll be able to figure it out. I think I'll head inside now and get Cami. She needs to get home and get ready for bed. And I'm sure Ruby could use a break from her."

They walked side by side with a safe distance between them. He opened the front door and held it for her. As she stepped inside, he heard Cami squeal.

"Daddy! Daddy!" His little blond angel threw her tiny body at him, wrapping her arms around his legs.

He reached down and scooped her up, an intense protective feeling coming over him as he hugged her. He watched as Tacy sat down on the sofa next to her aunt. It was the perfect opportunity for him to leave.

"Ladies, we'll be going now." He looked at Ruby, trying hard not to see the expression on Tacy's face. "Ruby, thank you for spending so much time with Cami and for seeing to her supper." He pretended to catch the kiss Ruby threw his way. Because he would never upset Ruby, he turned to Tacy and nodded. "Good night."

With that he carried his little girl out the door, stopping only for a second to make sure the door had caught and locked behind him. It was just his natural instinct to protect the ones he loved. Tacy Clark just happened to be in Ruby's house. It didn't mean anything. He ignored the funny feeling in his stomach, chalking it up to eating that hotdog too fast.

Chapter Seven

The buzzing of her old alarm clock startled her out of a deep sleep. Until the persistent buzzing had woken her, she'd been lost in a dream. She sat up in her old childhood bed, rubbing the sand from her eyes, the details of her dream still vivid. She'd been running through the orchards, looking for Uncle Jerry. Clad in a familiar pair of overalls, something she'd worn more than she would care to admit, she'd been weaving in and out of the dozens of apple trees, getting more distraught each time she failed to find her uncle. She'd been calling his name and in her arms had been her stuffed teddy bear, Beethoven.

As she sat in bed getting her bearings and rubbing the goosebumps that ran up and down her arms, she looked around the room. In the excitement of chasing her dreams, she'd forgotten to pack the old bear to take with her. Now as her eyes scanned the room, she couldn't find him. She made a mental note to ask Aunt Ruby where the bear had gone to. For now, she wanted to get up and get Ruby her breakfast before the woman had a chance to get to the kitchen on her own.

She'd been happy to spend a little time with her aunt last night after her dinner with Brody. After he and Cami had left, the two of them had enjoyed tea and cookies together. They'd reminisced about Uncle Jerry

74

and Tacy had been surprised to find that her aunt wasn't the only one with a tear in her eye. She had thrown herself so into her music that she'd blocked out any chance to think about the man who'd been like a father to her. For as long as she could remember she'd thought of him as her father.

After spending so much time with Lucy Aimes and her father, she began to wonder what it would be like to know her real father, her biological father. When she questioned her aunt and uncle, her aunt would just nod her head and look away. It was the only time she'd seen her uncle get angry. But he never yelled or carried on. He simply left the room and holed up in his little office alcove, leaving Tacy with her aunt who would gently tell her that her mother had chosen not to reveal her father's name. Seeing the tears in her aunt's eyes, she'd let it go, telling herself that when the time was right she'd find out what she wanted to know. For the last seven years, since she'd moved to the city, she'd made music her life. She breathed, ate, and slept for music. There was no time for anything else.

After helping her aunt into bed last night, she'd cleaned up in the kitchen, washing the plate and tea cups they'd used for their evening snack. Just as she'd gone to switch off the kitchen light, her eyes searched out her old violin perched in the corner. She wondered what her uncle would think of the shiny new violin she'd sold most of her belongings for after arriving in the city. She threw off the covers as if she were shaking away the old memories that were bombarding her. She jumped out of bed and reached for the robe she'd lain at the foot of her bed the night before.

Without even setting foot in the kitchen she

knew Aunt Ruby had beat her to the punch. She'd set her alarm clock to be sure she'd be up on time but it hadn't been early enough. The smell of chocolate chip pancakes filled her nose, bringing unexpected tears to her eyes. She hadn't eaten any of those since she'd left home.

"Aunt Ruby! I got up early so I could make you something." Her aunt stood in front of the stove as she'd seen her stand for as long as she could remember.

The pink floral robe and slippers were a first though, as her aunt and uncle always left their bedroom dressed for the day. It made her wonder if her aunt was trying to make an effort for her. She should be resting, she thought. Instead, her aunt turned around, a smile on her face, her gray hair slightly mussed from her sleep, another first.

"Oh, now, I wanted to make you a good home cooked breakfast. I'll bet you eat cold cereal. I made your favorite." She was scooping a half dozen pancakes from the griddle to a plate.

Tacy hurried over to grab the plate and save her aunt a trip to the table.

"I eat just fine. I'm here to take care of you, remember? I was planning to make you your favorite."

She saw the wistful look in her aunt's eyes and remembered a time when as a child she'd attempted to make her aunt a vegetable omelet. She'd gone through two dozen eggs and they'd ended up eating cold cereal. Her uncle had teased her about it for what seemed like days on end. She couldn't help but laugh out loud.

"I know what you're thinking, but honestly my cooking has gotten better. I think you'll be pleasantly surprised at supper tonight." She had every intention of cooking her aunt's evening meal.

She'd already crossed her own line yesterday when she'd asked Brody Porter for help finding apple pickers. And then she'd remembered her stranded car. Who else was there to ask for help getting it back home? Her words rang in her ears. She'd told the man they wouldn't be needing his help at all, and so far she'd gone to him for help with two things. Her irritation at the thought of Brody Porter with a cocky smirk on his face must have shown. Her aunt had a funny look on her face.

"I promise. I intend to make you a nice supper tonight. I'm going to spend the day making a few more phone calls and then I'll get out to the barn and have a look around. But I'll have plenty of time to cook."

Her aunt gave her a sheepish grin.

"What's wrong? Would you rather go out? I imagine you're getting pretty bored being cooped up here all the time. We can go somewhere and get supper out if you prefer."

"No, dear, it's not that. I'm actually fine with being home. I've always been a homebody. It's just that Saturdays are pizza nights here."

Tacy stared at her in shock. "Pizza nights?"

Her aunt latched on to the walker she'd parked in front of the refrigerator and maneuvered her way over to the table where Tacy had been standing with her plate in her hand. Thinking her food would be getting cold, Tacy sat down and put the plate on the table. Her aunt parked the walker in the corner by her old violin. Tacy jumped up to help her into her chair. Her aunt let Tacy guide her into the chair and let out a soft moan.

"Yes, dear. We've sort of started a new tradition

around here. On Saturday nights after Brody gets off work he brings home a pizza for Cami, myself and him. After pizza, we usually play the matching card game with Cami."

She stopped, but Tacy could see there was something else she wanted to say. She saw her aunt's cheeks color.

"I look forward to it all week long."

Tacy picked up her fork and knife and cut into the fluffy pancakes, the melted chocolate chips dripping down from them. She scooped a forkful into her mouth.

"Oh, well, that's fine then. Actually, maybe that'll give me a chance to practice while you three eat and play games together. I have an important audition coming up in a week and I need to be ready as soon as I get home."

Her aunt was sipping from a cup of coffee that sat on the table in front of her. Tacy sniffed the air, the familiar scent of the coffee her aunt and uncle had drank for years making her feel almost as if she'd never left. Her aunt put the cup down and swiped at her mouth with a paper napkin.

"Oh, Tacy, you'll have to join us for pizza. You have to eat too. You might even like to join us for a round of cards. Cami is such a sweet child. She...she reminds me of you a bit."

Tacy took more pancake in her mouth, feeling a flush of heat in her face.

"I was never a blond, Aunt Ruby." Why she said it she didn't know. She was just baffled that her aunt would think the little girl reminded her of herself at the same age. She didn't want to think that it was because the four year old didn't have a mother just as Tacy had lost her own mother as a three year old.

"Of course not, dear. But she reminds me of you. She's such an inquisitive, smart little girl. And she adores her father."

"Well, I don't know about that." She wanted to add 'I didn't even know my father', but she let it go.

"Oh, yes. You were such a smart little girl. And you loved your Uncle Jerry. From the time you started walking you followed him everywhere. You loved being out in the orchards with him. You remember?"

Yes, she remembered. She remembered why she wanted that first pair of overalls. Because Uncle Jerry wore overalls and she wanted to be just like Uncle Jerry. She remembered working in the orchards every year alongside him. She remembered riding in his truck to the hardware store to help pick up supplies. She remembered running to him crying when a boy at school, John Lerner, had called her a boy. She'd been such a tomboy. That was until she'd met Lucy Aimes. She shook her head, forcing her thoughts to change direction. Her aunt was staring at her, waiting for an answer.

"Yes, of course. I remember that." She got up and walked over to the sink where the tea kettle sat in the drainer. She turned on the water and filled the kettle. All that chocolate and syrup left her with a sandpaper feeling in her mouth. She dropped the kettle on the stove and turned towards her aunt.

"So, Brody Porter is raising Cami all by himself?" The question came out of her mouth before her inner sensor could squash it. Brody Porter and his daughter were none of her business.

"Yes. He's a good dad. He loves that little girl.

Anybody can see it just looking at the way that little girl runs to him. He's got a lot on his plate. It's not easy running your own business and raising a child by yourself."

"Well, I can see he's got you helping him out. He must be doing okay."

"Oh, it's more like who's helping who. For the little bit of watching I do for Cami, she gives me so much more. I really enjoy having a little one around the house again. Sometimes it's just too quiet here."

The words stung. Again, what she wasn't supposed to hear all those years ago came flooding back to her, echoing in her mind in her aunt's voice. Had her aunt forgotten what she'd said back then? She'd told Uncle Jerry she hadn't signed on to raise a child all those years ago. Tacy had heard her say it herself. She couldn't help but feel hurt hearing her aunt gush about a little girl who wasn't her own.

The screech of the whistling tea kettle filled the awkward empty silence in the room. Tacy shut off the burner. She opened a cabinet and grabbed a mug. The metal tin where her aunt had kept tea bags was exactly where it had been all her life. She dropped a tea bag in her mug and watched the steam rise as the hot water covered it.

"I'm glad you've got company." It wasn't what she wanted to say. If she could have said what she wanted, she would have asked her aunt why she had said what she'd said all those years ago. But she didn't have time for that. She was here for one thing and one thing only - to get that harvest picked and ready for the festival. And not because Brody Porter had summoned her to do it. She was going to do it for Uncle Jerry.

Maybe if she got that done she would be able to let this guilt go.

~

Lucy Aimes-Hurley wasn't her usual chatty self. Though he'd told her to be at the shop for opening at six, he'd been surprised to find her there when he opened the back door at five in the morning. When he'd asked about it, she brushed it off just saying she thought with the picking season upon them he might need a little more prep help to get the day started. They'd worked in near silence for the hour, a silence he wasn't sure what to think of.

The welcome chime of the bells on the shop door broke the silence as the early birds stumbled in for their morning caffeine. They worked well together, staying in sync as they churned out coffee after coffee while they managed to stay on top of warming cinnamon buns, croissants and chunks of fresh chocolate swirled pound cake. At times it seemed like the customers were three deep, pushing to get closer to the counter, yelling for added touches to their gourmet drinks while others grabbed a complimentary newspaper and lingered at a table. Among the early customers were mothers with small children in tow, some with infants in strollers, the haggard look of lack of sleep in their eyes, hair ruffled in an 'I don't even care anymore' way.

"How's he doing, Susan?" He asked one mom in particular.

Susan Donovan had been trying to have a baby for more than ten years. She'd given up at one point. Then, like a biblical miracle, she found herself pregnant. She was forty five years old. She'd been an advertising executive in Newark, New Jersey at the time she'd found out. Now instead of custom suits and sleek black heels, her wardrobe consisted of stretch jeans, formula stained tees and hopefully a pair of sneakers that matched. A somewhat mussy pony tail bobbed up from the stroller where she'd been trying to appease her three month old with a binky.

"Same old, same old, Brody. I sure could use your afternoon Power Punch."

Brody raised his eyebrows. "At ten in the morning? Wow. That must have been some night you had." He gave her the thumbs up sign and started on her request.

He reached in to display case and grabbed a croissant and dropped it on a plate. He pushed the plate over to her and put the hot drink in her waiting hands. Without hesitation, she tore off the lid and gulped the hot liquid down. Brody cringed. He knew people didn't know how hot the temps on the coffee machines ran, but he wondered if they would gulp it down like that if they knew. Susan didn't even blink.

"Ok, usual for the coffee and the croissant is on me. You earned it." He patted away the extra money she offered.

She let out a deep breath. "Thanks, Brody. You're the best. You're so understanding. Wish I could get my husband to take some lessons for you, but he's busy sleeping right now." Juggling her plate and coffee, she pushed her stroller over to a corner table. She dropped down into a sunny chair.

Brody saw the binky bobbing lightly in the baby boy's mouth. Peace at last, he thought.

With a lull at the counter, he decided to get out

on the floor and wipe down tables. It was also the perfect time to talk to his high school trio about making a little money. After talking to Tacy about looking around for pickers, he realized the solution was right under his nose. Jack Pritchett, Erin Dunley and Mary Ellen West were all high school juniors and each of them had inquired about working for him in the past year. He liked them all. Problem was he only had enough room on the payroll for one person besides himself. Lucy Aimes-Hurley had a lot more flexibility in her schedule than three high school kids. And to top it off, sometimes she bailed him out with Cami when he was in need of getting her picked up or dropped off.

Right now his little angel was probably waking up at Lizzy Hart's house where he'd left her, tucked tight in Lizzy's daughter's bed. With her daughter away at college, Lizzy had gone back to work at the church preschool. What better person to leave his daughter with than her preschool teacher? Cami loved Lizzy and Lizzy, still suffering from an empty nest having had only one child, lived for having the little girl spend time with her.

Jack, Erin and Mary Ellen were parked at a corner table at the opposite end of Susan and her baby. Good thing for that, since the trio often got raucous, their laughter echoing from the modern metal beamed ceiling. He'd hate for them to wake up Susan's baby boy.

"Hey guys, I've got something I wanted to talk to you about." He grabbed the empty chair at the table for four and made himself comfortable. Three sets of eyes looked hopefully at him.

"Nah, I still can't give you a job, but if you're

interested in a few days' pay I know of someone who can." He watched them put down their drinks and give him their full attention.

Mary Ellen, their leader it seemed, piped up first, her short bob of hair so dark he could only guess she dyed it that black.

"A few days' pay? Is it here? What would we have to do?" She tapped a long shiny red nail on the table as she waited.

"Yeah, what's it all about?" Jack chimed in, puffing out his chest as if to prove he was in charge of the group.

Brody stifled the urge to laugh.

"Ok, it's not here. I'm trying to get a group of people together to pick apples for the annual harvest festival. You'd be working at Hill Top Orchards for Miss Ruby. I don't know what the pay is, but I can give you her niece's number and you can ask her yourselves."

The three sets of eyes darted amongst themselves. Brody got the message.

"Ok, you talk it over amongst yourselves. And if you decide you're interested, come up to the counter for the number." He tucked his chair in and headed for the counter where Lucy was filling a box of pastries for a young couple. Bits and pieces of their conversation wafted in the air as he stacked baking trays to return to the back room.

As he'd guessed, they were newlyweds heading for a B&B just outside Hill Top. As they asked Lucy where they could go apple picking, he thought of Tacy. In his mind he crossed his fingers that his loyal coffee sipping trio would take him up on the job opportunity he'd offered. A small town wasn't exactly the land of opportunity for working age teens and many of the mom and pop shops gave first dibs to their own kids and family members. The job would likely end within a week's time as they were only harvesting enough apples for the annual festival. If they said no, he'd have to talk to a few of the older people around town and see if he got any interest.

He balanced a half dozen large baker's trays on his right shoulder and headed to the back room. He double checked the ovens to be sure they were off. Since they didn't serve anything more than breakfast type foods, the ovens were shut down early in the day.

It was another reason he just had to pull off this apple picking season at Ruby's. The preschool survived on funds donated from the annual harvest festival. The event was one of the few times of the year when people from all over would come to buy apples. If Ruby's orchards didn't get harvested, the festival would be sorely lacking in funds. And that meant the preschool wouldn't be able to offer a full day program, something that all his plans hinged on. With a full day, he wouldn't have to worry about shuttling Cami between Lizzy and Ruby. And he could finally expand his menu with some of the great lunch foods he'd been waiting to offer his customers.

No matter how much he tried to picture his sweet little girl, an image of Tacy standing beside her Beetle kept intruding. He had to wonder if she'd managed to find anybody on her own. As great an idea as it was, his trio of teens wouldn't be enough hands to harvest hundreds of apples. If Tacy couldn't come up with pickers from her uncle's list, who else could she get?

He dropped the trays into the tub sized sinks and turned on the water. His jaw clenched as he remembered her talking about the short time she planned on staying, the way dark strands of hair fell on to her forehead when she turned from Lucy to himself as they ate at the cafe. A different feeling came over him and it irritated him even more.

The last thing he needed was to get involved with another woman on her way to something else. Once they got these pickers together and the apples were ready for the festival, that would be the end of it. Tacy had her music to get back to and he had his life here in Hill Top. He knew from experience that a woman like Tacy would never let anything come before what she wanted. And from the way she'd let her relationship lapse with her aunt, he knew family was not on her ten year list.

# Chapter Eight

Tacy's plan to spend the day reacquainting herself with her uncle's barn and property had been slightly waylaid. Coming home four years after her last visit, it hadn't occurred to her how much change she would encounter. Though Aunt Ruby was only in her early seventies, Tacy felt as if her aunt had aged overnight.

After cleaning up the breakfast dishes in the kitchen and getting her aunt settled with her knitting on the porch, she'd wandered back into her uncle's office, hoping to make a few more calls for pickers. After leaving a half dozen or so messages, she'd felt hopeful and decided to head outside. Expecting to dig into some physical work, she'd headed to her room to put her hair into a ponytail when she'd spied her aunt's hamper overflowing by the linen closet. Thinking she'd come home to cook and care for her aunt, it never occurred to her that there would be chores that her aunt had neglected due to her limited mobility.

She'd dragged the hamper down to the basement, its bottom thumping in protest the entire flight down. Grateful she'd remembered the light switch at the top of the stairs, she had no problem navigating the cluttered basement. She dumped the first load of clothes into the washing machine and started it as she glanced around the musty smelling space.

As a child she had loved to follow Uncle Jerry down the creaky stairs to what she pretended was some far away magical land. Her uncle would spend time looking for something or other as she would snake her way between high columns of corrugated boxes filled with what, she never knew. Against one wall was a wooden work table that her uncle would often bring small appliances to for repair.

Tacy stared at the table now, an old toaster sitting with its guts splayed in front of it, mortally wounded, whether it was broken or forgotten she wasn't sure. The same columns of boxes were there still sealed with dark brown packing tape. As a child she'd never thought twice about the boxes. Now as a grown woman she couldn't help but wonder why someone had failed to label the contents of each box. She couldn't remember ever seeing her aunt or uncle open any of them.

As the washing machine hummed along happily doing what it was called to do, she thought briefly about opening a carton out of curiosity. Then she remembered how much work she had ahead of her. She wasn't here to clean out a basement, she reminded herself.

She'd taken the steps back up to the main floor of the house two at a time. After the laundry she was headed for her uncle's office when she noticed something she hadn't noticed yesterday when she'd arrived. Pretty much every surface in the house was coated in a fairly thick layer of dust. And so she'd gone to the supply closet off the kitchen and took out her aunt's cleaning caddy, complete with feather duster and polish. From the living room she attacked the bathroom and her aunt's bedroom, her eyes taking in all of the framed pictures her aunt had spread throughout the room. Most of the pictures were of her aunt and uncle, and several were of Tacy at different ages in her life, but the one that made her lose time was a large framed picture of her mother, Fern.

She'd seen plenty of pictures of her mother, a woman who baffled her. Tacy looked nothing like her dirty blond haired mother. As she'd gotten older and curious about her mother, she had asked her aunt why she had the dark brown hair she had. Her aunt had made a funny face, but after Tacy persisting she'd finally offered that she'd probably gotten her hair color from her father. She'd been about seven years old then and the answer had spurred her on. She'd wanted to know what most children who had never met their father wanted to know. Who was her father? What did he look like? Why wasn't he there, living with her like the other children's dads did? She didn't understand why her aunt had gotten upset and she'd gotten no answers.

A few years later, when she was on the cusp of teen-hood, her uncle had told her a little bit about the mystery man who was her father. It hadn't been much. According to her uncle, her father had been a migrant worker, a picker from Veracruz, Mexico, passing through one season. He told Tacy how he'd seen the looks passing between Fern and her father, a man who went by the name of Severo, though there was really no way to know who he was. Her uncle never asked any of the pickers to fill out any paperwork.

Like many other orchards, he supplied them all with a place to sleep, a community sleeping area, and one meal a day. He had tried to warn her mother that it would be a mistake to get involved with Severo. He was passing through and when the season was over, and the pay gone, he would be on his way.

But her mother had been what her aunt had called a 'wild child' and she'd tossed caution and her uncle's words to the wind. Two months after Severo had left to pursue work in Florida, her mother had found herself pregnant with Tacy.

That was all her uncle had offered her, whether because she was only thirteen years old or because there wasn't much more to offer. But she had learned to be content with the information and accept that she would never know the man who was her father.

Now it was a little before five o'clock and she was just opening the barn doors. She knew from experience that she only had about two good hours of daylight left. Struggling to pull the doors open all the way, a mingling of scents assaulted her nostrils. Her aunt had cautioned her that the barn would be in a serious state of disrepair. She'd also told her that it had been a long time since any animals had occupied the space. The rank odor that permeated the air disagreed.

Tacy took a few cautious steps inside, her eyes like a lighthouse light, going around the room vigilantly, not sure what she expected to see. Remnants of hay was scattered about the dirt floors. The entire right side wall was filled with iron pegs that held apple baskets in the common sizes pickers worked with - quarter peck, half peck and full peck. Most of the baskets were the same, made of a light washed-out wood with wire and wooden spool handles to make for easy carrying. Along with the baskets were dozens of harvest aprons, a typical apron style except instead of one or two small pockets in front, the entire width of the apron was a pocket reinforced to hold the weight of a few dozen apples. A few familiar handmade cider presses sat abandoned against the wall.

The ghosts of pickers past seem to tell a story from the forgotten folded card tables and folding chairs that leaned against wooden barrels, their legs laced with spider webs. Tacy could still picture those tables and chairs strewn about the barn, pickers coming and going, stopping for a drink of water or to escape the hot sun they worked under for more than ten hours a day.

Uncle Jerry's tractor was still hitched to the long wagon he drove out to the orchard to pick up the bushels of picked apples. The once bright blue wagon was now faded, the name Hill Top Orchards painted on the side almost completely gone. She winced at the comparison of her uncle being gone too.

She'd driven the tractor several times for her uncle, her protest that she might take down a tree or two, having fallen on deaf ears. Her uncle had believed she could do anything. The memory gave her a boost of confidence.

Maybe she really could do this. If she could just hire a team of pickers, together they just might be able to pull it off. She walked over to the tractor and touched the steering wheel, almost seeing Uncle Jerry's gloved hand clutching it the way he did.

Impulsively, she jumped into the seat. She'd forgotten how it felt to sit perched up high in that seat. The key was sitting in the ignition. She guessed it probably had been for the last four years. This was Hill Top, after all. There was no need to worry about anyone stealing anything. Most folks still didn't lock their doors, as if it were still the nineteen fifties. Without expecting much, she turned the key, pumping the gas once as her uncle had taught her.

She was beaming. Why an old forgotten tractor coming to life would feel like such an accomplishment was beyond her. Compared to the dozens of auditions she'd gone to it was nothing. And yet it felt like the start of something big. *You've watched one too many hero movies.*

There she sat on top of the world, getting a good view of the entire barn. Thinking it would be a good idea to take it for a spin, she climbed down quickly and made her way to the back of the tractor where the wagon was hitched to it. Funny the things you remember. Without missing a beat, she released the wagon from the tractor and jumped back into the seat. With the doors wide open and ready, there was no reason not to give it a go. She pressed down on the gas gently and began steering her way out of the barn. She surprised herself at how smooth it went. Once out of the barn she turned right and drove past the small fenced corral that once housed her aunt's horse, Petunia. Seeing the trees in the distance, she picked up her pace and headed for the orchards, enjoying the way the wind caught her hair.

Within minutes, she was in the midst of the fifty acre apple orchard. With about eighty trees per acre, Tacy was still in awe today thinking about the possibility of close to four thousand trees bearing apples every season. Of course it had been a long time since her uncle had run a season to the hilt, as he called it. And with four years of neglect, she was almost certain many of the trees had long since died or at the least could no longer bear fruit.

Carefully weaving in between, she angled the tractor as close to the base of the trees as she could, throwing her head back so she could get a look at what she would be dealing with. The sweet scent of ripe apples permeated the air. She thought of the apple scented candle she had back in her apartment. No candle or room spray could match the strong, heady scent of fresh ripe apples just waiting to be snatched from the trees.

She frowned seeing that more apples were on the ground than clinging to the branches. Once they hit the ground, the apples were no longer suited for market stands. If her uncle were alive, he would have gathered as many as he saw fit and used them for press. Bruised, fallen apples were usually saved for juicing. Still, there were many apples to be picked and she wished she'd grabbed her uncle's clipboard with the diagrams of the orchards so she could figure out which kinds of apples she would yield for the annual harvest festival.

Remembering that she was doing all this for the harvest festival made her remember Brody Porter, something she had planned on not thinking about today.

Pulling her phone from her pocket, she saw it was a little after six o'clock. She'd be losing the sunlight that she needed to guide her around the property soon. She was in no rush to return to the farmhouse to find Brody and his little girl eating dinner with her aunt.

She'd tried to find reasons why she couldn't join the happy trio for their Saturday night pizza. No matter what she'd come up with, her aunt had managed to come back with a reason why she just had to join them. The little girl was adorable, she had to admit. And her father was just as cute if not more appealing. But the last thing she needed was to get involved with a man like Brody Porter.

And besides that, she would be heading back to the city very soon. She had only enough time and energy to handle what she'd come here to do. Feeling like part of a happy family wasn't on the agenda.

Without a flash light, she knew she needed to get the tractor and herself back to the barn. Feeling like an old pro, she turned the tractor around, careful not to hit any trees, and headed back to the barn.

It took her a little longer than she'd intended to park the tractor back the way she'd found it. Satisfied, she walked out of the nearly dark barn and prepared to do battle with the heavy barn doors she'd have to close up by herself. She'd always had extra hands when it came time to pull the heavy wooden doors closed. She was sorry she'd made such an effort to pull them so wide open to begin with. Yet, there was no way she would have gotten the tractor out otherwise.

Feeling the beginnings of beads of sweat on her top lip, she tightened her grip on one door and threw her body into it, pulling it with all her might. In her mind, she made a note to find the grease her uncle had used on the barn door hinges. There had to be an easier way. With one door closed, she leaned against it for a moment to catch her breath. Wiping her forehead with the back of her hand, she bolstered up her strength for door two.

With the barn locked tight, Tacy walked along the once clear path that led from the barn to the farmhouse. Her uncle had prided himself on keeping the dirt path free of brambles and weeds. Now with him gone for four years, the brambles and weeds had encroached the pathway. Catching her ankle on a thick root of some kind, Tacy had to watch every step she took. As she cleared the pathway, she stood in the big round driveway where her ailing car sat lifeless. Behind it, a frog green pick up was parked so close, the two vehicles bumpers almost touched.

*That Brody Porter sure has a lot of gall.* From the window, the soft glow of lights in the living room told her that the Saturday night pizza party was underway. The hairs on her arms bristled. She blamed it on the cool change in the air, a sure sign that fall was in full swing.

She started up the driveway and headed for the porch steps. She had no interest in eating pizza with Brody, so why her hand picked at a few stray strands of hair was beyond her.

~

Tacy Clark sure didn't look like a professional musician. She stepped into the dining room wearing what was clearly a pair of men's dirty industrial strength coveralls and an expression that said she'd forgotten she had them on. She looked frozen in the opening between the dining room and the hallway. He stared at her as she ran a hand through her dark brown hair, a flush of color spreading across her face.

"Sorry to interrupt. I just wanted to let you know I'm back from the orchards." As quick as she'd entered the room, she spun around to leave. Brody didn't have to make the first move. Ruby made the invitation to join their Saturday night pizza party.

"Tacy, dear, why don't you go clean up then come back and join us? I know you've been busy, but you have to eat. I'll bet Cami and Brody would love the company too."

Brody felt as hot as the red flush of color on Tacy's face. He picked up his slice of pizza and bit into it a little more enthusiastically than needed. Glancing at Cami to check her plate, he was happy to see his daughter had eaten most of the slice Ruby had plopped on her plate. It didn't matter one way or the other whether Tacy ate with them or not. He grabbed a napkin and took a swipe at Cami, one ear slightly tuned in to the women as they chatted. It seemed she'd decided to clean up and join them. He took the napkin he'd swiped Cami's mouth with and gave his own a quick check.

He'd ditched his usual work wardrobe of black t-shirts and jeans in favor of a blue and green plaid long sleeve shirt and blue khakis. As he pulled into Ruby's driveway, he almost thought about turning back home and changing. Sure enough, Ruby had commented on how nice he looked this evening. He imagined his own face was as beet red as Tacy's was. He didn't want Tacy thinking he'd dressed for her. It was just another Saturday night pizza party like he, Cami and Ruby had started when he'd first gotten settled in Hill Top.

He'd been so busy analyzing his clothes he hadn't heard her come back into the dining room. He looked up and dropped his napkin. She was wearing a pale blue sweater and a pair of jeans with a pair of white sneakers. He didn't need to notice every detail like he did.

"Tacy, you can sit next to me and Dad." Cami's little voice broke the awkward silence, but if anything it made things more awkward for him.

Her eyes met his as if to check with him whether it was okay. Out of the corner of his eye he saw a slight twitch at the corner of Ruby's lips. He ignored her and stood up. He pulled out the empty chair next to his daughter and gestured for her to sit down. The way she smiled made him wonder what she was really like. The confident girl who'd stood her ground on that road, giving him fair warning about a gun he doubted even then that she had, just the day before seemed almost unsure of herself today.

With her seated, he tucked her chair in and sat back down, grateful for Cami's little body between them. He thought he saw her hand shake as she reached into the pizza box and grabbed a slice. Thinking there wasn't much to the girl, he was taken back that she chose one of the bigger slices in the box. He watched her take a hearty bite until her eyes met his. He rearranged his plate and glass. It was Cami, once again, who broke the silence.

"I like your violin!"

The simple sentence shot out of her so that all three adults looked up at the little girl. It was Ruby who spoke first.

"Cami, have you been playing with that violin in the kitchen? Remember, honey, I told you not to touch it. Those things are so fragile."

Brody caught the apologetic look she shot at Tacy.

"Miss Ruby, I'm sorry about that." He turned his attention to his little girl. He wasn't much of a disciplinarian. Maybe it was because he felt she'd already gotten a raw deal not having a mother so young.

"Sweetie, remember we talked about touching

97

what's not yours. This is Miss Ruby's house so if she told you not to touch that violin you have to listen." He was a sucker. He gae her his strictest look, but those rosebud lips pursed at him with that cocked head, and just did him in.

"Oh, please, it's no big deal. I don't mind if she'd like to play with it. I haven't touched it since...in years, so I'm glad it's not gathering dust sitting there." Tacy was smiling at Cami to which the little girl clapped her hands in happiness.

"I just touched some of the strings. I want to play a violin like you when I grow up." A wisp of blond hair fell in her eyes as she jutted out her chin with a determined look.

Brody heard Ruby chuckle, but his eyes were on Tacy. She was still smiling at the little girl as she patted her arm.

"Do you like music?" Her attention was one hundred percent on Cami.

Blond locks flapped back and forth as she shook her head.

"Yes. I listen to Miss Ruby's radio on the porch and at school I play the tambourine when we march in class."

The pride in her voice took Brody by surprise. He had no idea his own daughter loved music like that. He beamed with pride.

"Well, if that's the case then I'm going to have to give you some lessons on that violin. What do you say we finish up eating, clean up for Miss Ruby, and I teach you a few notes after we're done?"

He'd never gotten Cami to do anything as fast as Tacy had that very moment. He followed Ruby out to the living room while the two ran about the table picking up plates and silverware, his daughter heading eagerly to the kitchen. Within what seemed like minutes the four of them were seated in the living room, his daughter beaming as she held the violin in her hands. She handed it to Tacy and sat down on the storage bench under the front window.

"First, you have to learn how to hold the violin so that you're able to move your hands in a way that creates the right notes at the right time."

Brody watched as Tacy tucked the worn violin under her chin, positioning the neck of the instrument in the web between her thumb and forefinger. She pointed her free hand to the bow in the case and his daughter eagerly handed it to her. As much as he tried to keep his eyes on his daughter's reaction, he couldn't help but stare at Tacy. Her eyes were closed. He relaxed and took her all in, not even glancing to see if Ruby had noticed. He wasn't much for fancy music. He preferred country himself, but he had to agree with Ruby. Tacy was a gifted musician.

He was mesmeroized by the shadow moving across her face, created by the motion of the bow's back and forth movement in the dim light, losing track of his dinner companions. He was entranced. Her dark wavy hair dangled on her forehead as she kept her face down, focused intently on her music. It was at least five minutes before he noticed his foot was keeping time to the beat. When she stopped playing he let out his breath. Taking a cue from his daughter, not wanting to be the first, he clapped his hands. The flush of color in her face, the way she swiped at the fallen waves of hair in her eyes, caught his breath.

Cami jumped up and ran over to Tacy. Grateful for the distraction, he got up and stretched his legs, turning his attention to the window so he could get control of himself again. He'd made a promise to himself that he would never lose it again.

## Chapter Nine

She couldn't remember the last time she'd slept so soundly. If it weren't for the phone ringing she suspected she would have slept for another hour easily. But the ringing phone had her running for the kitchen to prevent her aunt from trying to hurry out of bed to answer it.

"Hello?" Still groggy, she dropped down on the old metal step stool under the wall phone. She'd spent many a night perched on the stool, the curly phone cord twisted around her fingers as she and Lucy chit-chatted about their school day.

"Tacy? Did I wake you?"

The husky voice sounded as unsure as she felt. Brody Porter's distinctive deep voice made her feel warm, despite the cool October morning air coming in the open window. It amazed her that in this day and age people actually left their windows unlocked at night, let alone open.

"Uh, no. I'm awake. Is something wrong?" An image of Cami came to mind. She'd really enjoyed spending time with the little girl. She refused to think about her father. The thoughts that ran through her head were too distracting.

"No, no. I hate to call so early on a Sunday morning, but I wanted to tell you that I've got three of the local high school kids willing to pick apples. They're high school juniors and they're regulars at my shop. Nice kids. I'm sure they'll be great."

Tacy rubbed the sand out of her eyes, hoping it would help her snap out of her sleep fog. She swiped a lock of hair from her eyes and twirled the springy yellow cord between her fingers, like she was a schoolgirl once again.

"That's terrific. I appreciate that, but don't they have classes? I'm planning on getting back out to the barn today so I can clean things up and get everything ready. I wanted to start tomorrow, if it's possible. From the scent in the air, I know those apples need to get picked right away." She strained to hear Cami's little voice piping up in the background. She was almost certain she heard the little girl say her name. A butterfly-like feeling filled her stomach. She was acting like a school girl.

"Don't worry about classes. It's administrative conference week so it's perfect timing. If you'd like I can come on over and give you a hand with that clean up. I've got the whole day free and it's only fair I give you a hand." She heard him suck in his breath. "After all, I did drag you back here to take this on and...well, you were right. I really do need this festival to be a success. You know for Cami and all."

Despite her lightweight t-shirt and sleeping pants, Tacy fanned herself with her free hand. He was apologizing for the email. Why she would be flattered was beyond her. It wasn't like he was complimenting her. He was probably feeling guilty.

"I understand. I imagine if she were my little girl I would have done the same thing. Sure, if you want to come on over and help out. But what about the coffee shop?"

"It's Sunday. With the exception of the cafe, there isn't a store open on Main Street. This is Hill Top you know." He chuckled, the whole time whispering something to Cami she couldn't quite make out.

After seven years of living in New York City, Tacy had forgotten that in some small towns across the country the Blue Law was still honored. Then it dawned on her that her aunt would probably want to get to church.

"I just thought of something. Aunt Ruby will probably want to get to church today. I'm not sure if she's been able to make it since her fall."

"Actually, last Sunday I dropped her off for the service with Cami. Since the preschool is part of the church a lot of Cami's little friends go on Sundays and she wanted to go too. It's been great having Ruby to do the things that my wife..." The words died on his lips.

Tacy waited in silence, not wanting to push him to talk about something that was probably painful. She listened to him tell Cami to go get dressed.

He cleared his throat and changed the subject. "If you'd like, I'll take Cami and Ruby to church so you can get started. Then after I've gotten them settled I'll meet you up at the barn. If that's okay with you."

Tacy pinched her wrist to snap herself back to reality. The butterflies were putting on an encore performance. This was just a day of work. A day of grimy work in a musty, smelly barn, wiping out cobwebbed baskets and hosing down ladders that hadn't seen the light of day in probably a decade. She was acting like she had a date. Acting like she'd never had a date with a guy before. She was being more than foolish.

After a close examination of the man while he ate his pizza Saturday night, she'd come to the conclusion that he was at least ten years older than her. And he was a father. The man had nothing on his mind except taking care of his daughter. *Listen to you! Toying with the idea of dating a guy like Brody Porter.* The deep questioning voice on the other end of the line snapped her out of her reverie.

"Tacy? Is that okay with you?"

"Uh, yes, sure. That works. Is the service time still the same? I'll see that Aunt Ruby is up and ready when you come to get her." And she'd also throw her flustered self into the shower so she could get her head on straight.

"It's an eleven o'clock service. I'm sure you're familiar with it from when you lived here. I'll come by and wait by the truck so I can help get Ruby down the steps and into the truck."

Tacy glanced at the clock, startled to find it was nearly ten already. It wasn't like Aunt Ruby to be lying in bed this late. Or was it? She had to admit she hadn't lived at home in seven years. *You haven't kept in touch.* She pushed away the guilt.

"I'll get her started right now. See you then." She set the receiver in the cradle and hopped off the step stool.

Before she did another thing, she was going to make sure Aunt Ruby was okay. After seeing her aunt around Cami, she was sure going to church with the little girl would get her up and going quick.

She stopped in front of her aunt's bedroom door

and gave it a firm rap.

"Come in, Tacy, dear."

She walked in to find her aunt fully dressed, clutching her walker while her feet struggled to slip into a pair of black sneakers.

Tacy rushed over and knelt down at her aunt's feet. "Let me help you with those."

"Oh, you're going to turn me into a lazy daisy, dear. I've been doing it this way for a few weeks. I can do it."

Nonetheless, she let Tacy take each foot and guide it into a sneaker. Satisfied they were secure on her aunt's feet, Tacy stood up. The dresses she remembered her aunt wearing to church years ago had been replaced by a simple floral sweater and gray slacks.

As if she could see Tacy taking notice of the change, she touched her arm." I've taken to a more casual look these days. I've learned the rules don't have to be so rigid." Her eyes searched Tacy's.

Tacy turned away and busied herself with picking up the pajamas at the end of her aunt's bed.

"I'll probably run another load of laundry later today when we're done with the barn."

The expression she couldn't make out on her aunt's face previously changed to one of surprise.

"We? I'm going to guess Brody is going to give you a hand today?"

"Yes, he is. If I get everything ready we can get the crew of pickers started tomorrow. Oh, and he's going to pick you up so you can go with Cami to church this morning. I thought you'd like that. Are you feeling up to it?" The light dancing in her aunt's eyes was answer enough.

"Wonderful. All I need to do is get us girls some breakfast and I'll be ready to go." Aunt Ruby grabbed her walker and took steady sure steps toward the door.

Tacy ran up behind her, her hands up just in case she should need to steady her as she made her way down the hall. She let her aunt inch her way through the kitchen doorway and then jumped ahead of her.

"I was thinking of scrambling up some eggs this morning for you. Let's get you a full stomach. I can take my food with me to the barn and pick while I work. I need as much time as possible to get ready for the pickers." Tacy reached into the cabinet under the sink where her aunt's pots and pans were nestled in one another.

She smiled, remembering the silly games she'd played with her uncle, in particular on Sunday mornings he wasn't going out to work the barn and had time to play. She'd empty all the pots and pans on the kitchen table and curl up inside the big cabinet, closing the door on herself so he'd never guess. How young she'd been to not even figure that he'd see the misplaced pots and pans and know where she was at once.

"Tacy, I'm going to get as big as a pig with her piglets if you keep on spoiling me like this."

The words belied her actions as she let go of her walker and sat down at the table. This was an Aunt Ruby she didn't recognize.

"Well, it'll make up for all the cooking you did for me all those years."

She'd never thought she was a spoiled child. At least not as far as her aunt was concerned. It was her Uncle Jerry who'd made her feel like she was special. It only became more obvious as she grew older and noticed the difference when her aunt was with her.

She grabbed the cooking spray and pushed down harder than need be on the nozzle. A gust of oily liquid flooded the pan. Feeling herself grow red, she reached for a paper towel and wiped the excess away, tossing the greasy towel into the pail besides the refrigerator. She glanced at her aunt but the woman was fiddling with her small white pearl earrings Tacy remembered her uncle giving her aunt for Christmas long ago. She glanced at the clock and almost dropped the spatula. It was already ten thirty. She'd forgotten to ask Brody what time he'd be outside, but if they wanted to make the service on time, she was pretty sure he'd be arriving soon.

"Eggs coming right up!" She said it more to reassure herself than her aunt, who seemed pleased just sitting there waiting for her food.

Considering the frenzy beginning to rise in the form of a flush of heat and slippery hands from too much cooking spray, the plate of eggs she placed in front of her aunt didn't look half bad. How much damage could you do to scrambled eggs? Her aunt dug in while she quickly washed and rinsed whatever she'd used to cook. She wanted to leave the kitchen neat. It would be one less thing she had to do later tonight when she finished up with what she was sure would be a grimy job out in the barn. And she'd have to come up with dinner for Aunt Ruby and herself on top of that.

Satisfied with the empty sink, she reached over and pulled open the refrigerator. A small plastic container housed the remains of the food she assumed Aunt Ruby and Cami had dined on Friday night. She closed the refrigerator door and poked in the freezer. There were just a handful of items. She made a mental note to get to Dunley's Mini Mart for some groceries some time tomorrow. Maybe when the pickers were settled in she would have a little time to go and come right back. Spying a pack of chopped beef, she grabbed it and laid it in the sink.

"It's getting kind of late so I'll check for Brody Porter and Cami. You take your time and when you're ready I'll help you out to his truck."

She left her aunt in the kitchen and headed to the living room. She stood in front of the big picture window and spotted her car, reminding her of yet another chore she had to take care of. Within seconds a noisy frog green truck came rumbling up the driveway. A tiny blond head in the passenger seat was bobbing excitedly. As they pulled around and behind her Beetle, a little hand poked out of the wind and waved to her. Tacy waved back and headed to the front door. She stepped out onto the porch and waited for Brody to kill the ignition and step out.

"Hi there!" She nodded to Brody and gave Cami a big wave. "Aunt Ruby will be ready in two seconds. She's just finishing up eating. I'll go and get her."

"No rush. Everyone at church knows Ruby's on a walker, so if she's late I'm sure it won't matter. Doubt she'll set tongues to wagging." He flashed a genuine smile at her.

Tacy smiled and hurried back inside, more so he wouldn't see the goosebumps on her arms than to get Aunt Ruby.

Still feeling a bit flustered, she wrapped her arm around Aunt Ruby and helped her out onto the porch.

Just as she was about to help her down the steps, Brody ran up the half dozen steps and reached out, his bare arms surprisingly tanned for a guy who worked in a coffee shop all day. Her eyes followed a muscled arm as he grasped Ruby's arm and pulled her against his body. Feeling as if she were an intruder, she followed behind them. Inside the truck Cami was straddling the gear shift, waiting for 'Miss Ruby' to 'come in'. Tacy watched as Brody settled her aunt in the seat. He turned to Cami.

"You know you can't sit on Miss Ruby's lap until her boo boo is all better, little miss. You hop into the back seat and get your buckle on." He turned to Tacy, who'd been so involved in the exchange she jumped.

"Ok, so it looks like you have everyone taken care of. I'll just go back inside and get myself ready to head to the barn." She looked him in the eye, trying to steady her breathing.

"Sure thing. I'll meet you up there as soon as I get these girls in their pew." With that he hurried around to the driver's side and jumped in to his seat.

Tacy stepped back and the truck sputtered to life. As the three of them tore down the driveway, she stood with her feet planted in the ground. The early morning sun wasn't the only thing beginning to heat things up.

~

Tacy took her time making her way to Uncle Jerry's barn. It seemed so long since she'd enjoyed fresh air and beautiful scenery. Granted in the city she'd spent a little time when she could in local parks, but time was money, money she didn't have. The last few years especially she'd spent most of her time running from every audition or musical opportunity she could to be sure she could make her rent each month. The constant cycle of running to and from had left her almost numb to her surroundings. It felt good to walk in the fresh air and sun and actually notice what was around her. As a child, and later as a teen, she'd always loved being outdoors. She'd loved nothing better than to take her violin down to the orchards and sit under a tree and play for hours.

Now the music she loved to play just for the love of it had become a chore, something she only did for a paycheck. It was rare she picked up her violin these days just for the love of hearing the music.

She made a mental note to ask Brody if he would mind helping her clear the mile or so long pathway that led to the barn. It seemed a shame that they'd gotten so overgrown since her uncle's passing.

She watched as the mockingbirds playfully chased each other from tree to tree. She listened to the assortment of calls and cries and admired the rainbow of colors that the assorted wildflowers proudly displayed along the way. As she crunched along the rock embedded dirt road to the barn, she was grateful she'd thought to dig out an old pair of work boots from her childhood closet. They were one of the last few clothing items she'd bought before she'd moved away and she'd figured they'd fit.

She tugged open the barn doors, took a deep breath and grabbed on to pull them the whole way open. The morning sunlight bathed the barn in a glow that made the cobwebs and neglect even more noticeable. How clean was a barn really supposed to be? She stood hands on hips, debating on where to start when a familiar rumbling filled her ears. *That was fast!* She turned around to see Brody Porter climbing out of his truck, a smile spreading across his face.

"What?" She felt the hairs on the back of her neck bristle in defense.

"Nothing. I was just admiring your work attire."

She looked him up and down, making sure he saw her do so. She hadn't noticed what he'd been wearing earlier. The white plain t-shirt appeared to be one he wore for hard work, but even the stains couldn't make the wearer less appealing. She tried hard to avert her eyes from jeans that hugged two muscular legs. He sure didn't look like a coffee-making, Danish-baking kind of guy.

"What?" The word was said with a playful grin. Too playful.

Tacy reminded herself they had work to do. And probably lots of it. She turned away from him and pointed inside the barn.

"So, I thought maybe we'd start by hosing out all the baskets and shaking out the aprons. We'll need to make sure they're all in good shape. I'd hate to have to order anything because it probably would just delay the picking." As she started walking around the barn, her arms animated as she went, she felt his presence closely behind her. It was starting to get hotter than she'd expected. She wished she'd thought to bring along a few water bottles.

"No problem. Since you know the biz, you can just give me orders and I'll do whatever you want me to do."

He'd stepped in front of her now, eye to eye

with her. Without an all-out grin, it was hard for her to tell what he was thinking. Surprisingly, she found his full beard and mustache rather handsome. Up close like this he was better looking than she would have preferred him be.

"Okay. Let's get started by taking down all the aprons from the hooks and inspect them for any tears. If they look sturdy, shake them out and we'll stack them in the back of the big wagon. Uncle Jerry always rode the pickers and their aprons out to the orchards at the start of the shift." She watched his eyes as they studied the dozens of aprons hanging from the hooks on the wall. With a slow turn, his eyes were on her.

"Everything looks good to me."

His lips parted and perfectly straight white teeth stood out from the dark facial hair.

Feeling too warm, Tacy took a step back.

"Okay, well, I'll work this wall and you can work that wall. This way we'll get more done and be ready to move on to the next task."

Grateful for an excuse to move away from him, Tacy walked over to the wall she assigned herself and grabbed a handful of aprons. She dropped a bunch on the floor and held on to the first one for inspection, pretending to be deeply engrossed in her work. Out of the corner of her eye, she was relieved to see Brody doing the same.

~

It must have been the lingering summer heat. Brody didn't know what the matter with him was. He was playing games with Tacy, heading for dangerous grounds. He should know better than that. He was standing in the barn with a handful of aprons slung over one shoulder, turning one over in his hands as he checked for rips and tears as Tacy had told him to. It seemed to him that Jerry had left the barn in good shape, the only problem being cobwebs and dust accumulating from years of not being touched. He gave the tan canvas apron a good hard shake and laid it down, beginning a pile of good aprons that would be put in the wagon that was tucked behind the tractor. He'd mention repainting the faded blue wagon to Tacy. He could make out the words Hill Top Orchards on the side in white paint. If the paint in the barn was dried up, he'd run to the hardware store and get some. It seemed a shame not to spiff up the wagon for the festival. He was sure Ruby would like it too.

As he dropped a second and third canvas apron onto the pile, he glanced over at Tacy. He couldn't help but laugh at the sight of her, deep in inspection, her head peeking into the over-sized apron pocket she was inspecting. She must have heard his laughter. Her head popped up. Her face reddened as she laughed too.

Inspecting, shaking and stacking aprons hadn't taken long at all. He was standing alongside the wagon with dozens of aprons stacked neatly inside it. Thinking of how she'd mentioned hosing out the apple baskets, he looked around for signs of a hose. Just as his eyes found the lone spigot at the back wall, a spray of cold water hit him square in the chest.

"What the...?" He yelled as he jumped out of her aim.

The girl was a Dr. Jekyl and Mr. Hyde. One minute she was aloof and unfriendly, the next she was charming his little girl. She was laughing at him now, still clutching the nozzle of the hose in both hands.

With what he was sure appeared as a dopey grin, he approached her with both of his hands up in the air.

"Okay, okay. I surrender. You got me. I'm empty handed. Please don't shoot." Surprisingly, she nodded and handed him a basket.

"I'm sorry. I couldn't resist. I had an unfair advantage. How about I give you a turn with the hose, and then we get working on these baskets?" She laid the nozzle and hose in his hand and stepped back, her hands covering her face in preparation for a soaking.

He stared at her. He had another idea of what he'd like to do to her, but it didn't involve a hose and water. As she peeked through her hands, he had to fight the urge to pull her hands away and flat out kiss her on the lips.

"That's okay. I'll take that as payback for dragging you back home like I did. You take the hose. I'll hold the baskets." It came out a little too unfriendly. Maybe it was for the best. They were getting too close. He thought about Cami and how she never knew her mother. It was enough to cool him off, wet or dry.

"Let's get to work." He lifted a basket up for her to hose out. He saw a fleeting look of disappointment cross her face and then felt the force of water as her hand squeezed the nozzle of the hose hard.

He thought those would be the last words said between them after they'd hosed out about a dozen baskets. He was wrong. The water stopped. He looked up and found her staring at him.

"What?" His tone softened from how he'd spoken before.

"Would you like to join me for dinner tonight? I mean, just me."

He couldn't look away from those dark chocolate eyes. How had they escaped his notice before? Feeling like he'd need to wet his tongue with the hose, he shook his head.

"Sure. Why not?" Even though every fiber of his being was giving him a thousand answers why he shouldn't.

## Chapter Ten

There were no computers or laptops in Aunt Ruby's house. If Tacy had been taking the convenience of her smart phone for granted, that evening she was more than grateful for what it could do. Namely, search for a restaurant outside of Hill Top. After their hotdog dinner at Evie's Cafe, she wanted to find somewhere to eat where they wouldn't run into anyone she knew. Seeing Lucy after all these years had thrown her a bit.

A nostalgic feeling had come over her seeing her old best friend after so many years. She couldn't help but think about all the catching up they might have done if things had been different. But she'd left without even saying a word to her, Tacy figured Lucy was angry at her and rightly so.

The words had rushed out of her mouth faster than the water from the hose when she'd invited Brody to dinner. She hadn't even thought about it. At least so she thought. Before she could apologize for being silly, he'd accepted. After explaining to her aunt that Cami would be eating with her this evening, and not missing the twitch of her aunt's lips, she'd excused herself to her uncle's little alcove office, to use her phone to find somewhere they could eat.

She'd managed to find chicken stock, pasta and enough frozen vegetables to throw together homemade soup for her aunt and Cami's meal. There was also some bread and cheese for sandwiches. Too late to cancel, she could at least find a restaurant just outside of Hill Top where they could eat and not run into anyone she knew.

Her search had turned up a Chinese restaurant just twenty five minutes from her aunt's house. That was twenty-five additional minutes she'd have to spend alone with Brody on top of dinner. What on earth had she been thinking? She didn't even like the man. Now here she was looking for a place to have dinner with him alone. Maybe they'd be better off at Evie's.

Then she thought about the likelihood of running into someone. Small towns chatter and Hill Top was no different. If they ate dinner there again someone was bound to say something to Ruby about seeing them together a few times. Next thing you would know, people would be thinking they were a couple. And she was not here to couple with anyone.

It was already six o'clock and Brody would be arriving with Cami any minute. He'd left her to finish up at the barn so he could bring Cami home for a late lunch. He'd told her that after lunch he was going to be watching a movie with his daughter, her all-time favorite about a mermaid. Tacy could guess which one it was. He'd told Tacy they'd be by after they were cleaned up and ready for dinner.

She glanced at the small wooden clock above Uncle Jerry's desk. Time was speeding by and she hadn't made much progress. Chinese it would have to be. Any other options seemed further away and she didn't feel comfortable going that far from Aunt Ruby. She needed to spend more time with her aunt. Thinking of the next few days, she realized she was going to have to make a conscious effort to do so.

Her aunt was in no condition to come out to the orchards, but that was where she would be for several days. She'd have to make sure she made dinner for her aunt every night. And after dinner she'd ask her aunt what she would like to do. She did tell Brody she'd bring her aunt to his coffee shop one day. She made a mental note and decided to focus on the task at hand.

Tacy pulled out the few things she'd packed for her short visit to her aunt's. She'd planned on working the orchards when she'd thrown her clothes into the duffel bag. Now she regretted it. There wasn't one thing she could consider nice for an evening out. She stared at the closet in her old childhood bedroom. She couldn't possibly fit in anything in there. Besides that, anything she left behind was seven years old and no doubt out of style.

*Why not?* The same words Brody had said. As she pulled open the closet door and felt along the inside wall for the light switch, a panicky thought came to mind. He probably didn't want to join her for dinner. He'd only taken her to Evie's for those hotdogs to be nice. He'd probably heard the growling of her empty stomach. And now she'd put him on the spot with her crazy blurted out invitation and of course he would say yes. He did it for Aunt Ruby. He didn't want to hurt her aunt's feelings.

Her eyes scanned the familiar colorful contents of her closet. An assortment of wonky sweaters, t-shirts with crazy sayings on them, and a bunch of jeans hung exactly where she'd left them.

Then she spied it. The frilly, shine of satin

fabric glowing from inside the clear plastic bag the store had carefully covered it with. She'd bought it for a date with Donnie Hays. He'd invited her to a dance at his college over two hours away. It was right before she'd left Hill Top. At the last minute he'd call to say he had to cancel, that something had come up. She'd been so disappointed. So crushed. But those feelings were nothing like the ones she'd felt when she'd overheard Cathy Roseman talking to Denise Worth about the magical time she'd had at Donnie Hays' college dance. She'd left the dress in her closet untouched. She'd refused to talk about it to anyone. She was sure Aunt Ruby wouldn't understand. She'd made up her mind at that point, after hearing just a few stories about her mother's romance with her runaway father, that Aunt Ruby wouldn't understand heartache.

She fingered the plastic bag, a layer of dust encircling the hook of the hanger that clung to the pole. Seven years since she'd left home and the dress had never seen the light of day. She removed it from where it hung and brought it out of the closet. Standing in front of the full length mirror her uncle had hung on her bedroom wall, she gave the bag a gentle shake. Tiny dust particles tickled her nose. She rubbed at the tip of her nose, stifling the sneeze that threatened.

She didn't really need to go to all this bother. It was just dinner with her aunt's friend after a day of working together. If anything, they were going to talk about the next day's work. The three teens Brody had found to pick apples would be at the barn early the next morning. This was really just a business dinner.

She ripped the bag from the dress and gave it a firm shake. Time hadn't touched the peach colored fabric. It wasn't too dressy for a dinner out. And from the looks of the wrinkled contents of her duffel bag, it was all she had. She unzipped it and threw it over her head. As she had figured, it fit.

She looked at her reflection in the mirror. With a quick swipe of her hands, she arranged her shoulder length dark wavy hair. She'd already had her usual every day make up on, just a touch of blush and mascara. She was good to go.

Stepping into the kitchen, her eyes went wide as she spotted Cami sitting at the table, a bowl and plate in front of her.

"You look real pretty." The tiny face beamed with approval. She seemed much older than she imagined a four year old to be. Not that she'd had much experience with children.

"Thanks, Cami." Tacy saw her aunt's approving smile as she stirred the pot of soup Tacy had cooked an hour ago.

"Yes, I have to agree with Cami. You look lovely. Where are you two going for dinner again?"

"I'm not quite sure. I think a Chinese restaurant in Benton." She looked away from her aunt and glanced at Cami. "So, is your dad here?" She assumed he was waiting for her in the living room. Blond curls danced as the little girl shook her head emphatically.

"Nope. But he gave me this to give to you." A chubby hand held out an envelope. She stared at Tacy with an impatient look, waiting for her to take it.

Tacy flushed. How silly letting a child make her feel uncomfortable like that. Or the envelope in her hand.

"Oh, okay. Thank you." She took the card from

the child's hand. She caught the way her aunt's eyebrows arched in question as she walked out of the kitchen. She stood in the hallway, needing to get a little space from her inquisitive audience. The card inside the envelope read:

*Tacy, the path is clear and ready for you. Meet me at the barn. Brody.*

She stared at Brody's tiny print, almost wondering if he had Cami write it. She admonished herself in silence. A four year old probably couldn't write that much. And would he involve his daughter in his plan?

His plan.

In an effort to moisten a very dry mouth, she gulped. She was being ridiculous. There was no plan. They were simply having dinner together, an idea that had been hers to begin with. She leaned in the doorway to the kitchen, hoping to break away as quick as possible.

"It seems Brody wants me to meet him at the barn. Guess he has to show me something. We'll probably leave straight from there, so I'll let you two enjoy your dinner."

"Okay, dear. You and Brody have a wonderful time." Aunt Ruby was seated at the small round kitchen table, opening up a napkin for Cami, who was in turn showing her she could do it better.

Tacy stifled the urge to laugh and darted to the front door. She grabbed her purse that had been under the small wall table, and closed the door behind her.

As she headed down the porch steps and made her way to the pathway that led to the barn, she hesitated for a moment. It was growing darker, and unlike in the city, her walk wouldn't be lit by street lights and flashing store signs. She almost thought about going inside and grabbing a flashlight. But she didn't want to keep Brody waiting and it was a short walk. Once she got to the barn she'd be climbing into his truck and they'd be on their way.

Her jaw nearly dropped as she took her first step onto the path. The overgrown weeds and thorny bramble that had taken over the once clear dirt path were gone. All that remained was the dirt path itself which looked as if someone had raked it free of rocks and sticks. The foundation for a packed down dirt trail had been laid.

She navigated the path in her sandals with ease. In the early evening darkness, the wildlife that inhabited the surrounding forest were out of sight, most likely tucked in for their night's rest. But she'd been wrong about one thing. As she looked up at the black velvet night sky, her steps were lit by the bright light of stars unimpeded by skyscrapers as she'd grown used to in the city. But they were nothing compared to the glowing lights she spotted in the distance. Knowing there was very little lighting in the barn, she hurried along to see what was going on.

She stopped short as she approached the barn. Both barn doors were wide open. Unlike the normal lighting which in her uncle's barn would be two hanging bulbs and the lanterns they always carried when she was a child, a string of bright white lights were wrapped around four poles. And in the center area between the four poles was a small table and two chairs.

Tacy stepped closer until she was standing just

in the doorway. She stared at the linen table cloth and the china carefully set on the table. Two tapers glowed from empty wine bottles. Her eyes darted around the barn looking for Brody when a tap on the shoulder nearly stopped her heart. She spun around to find her face a little too close to Brody's, his dark brown eyes reflecting the light coming from the barn. She didn't miss the black jacket he'd thrown on over the white shirt and jeans he was wearing. It struck her as an odd mix of casual and elegance. She hated to admit it suited the occasion perfectly. *It's just dinner.*

"Wow. I thought I was taking you out to dinner." The words came out in a jumble, reflecting how she felt.

His mouth broke into a grin, his white teeth almost as bright as the lights that filled the barn.

"I thought about that and realized you probably won't have too many options. And being you're from the bright lights of the city I thought maybe you'd like this instead of Evie's Cafe and hotdogs."

She couldn't help but smile. This was so far from what she was expecting. She actually didn't know what she was expecting. She still couldn't figure out what she was thinking when she'd ask the man to join her for dinner. Before she could answer, he slipped his arm in hers and led her into the barn.

"Miss, your seat?" He made a sweeping gesture and helped her into a folding chair. Once she was seated, he pulled his own seat out and sat down.

"This is beautiful. I don't know what to say." She didn't. This was a side of Brody Porter she hadn't expected.

"Say that you like lemonade because it's all I

had at home. As I told you, pretty much everybody is closed on Sundays in Hill Top. I would have brought a bottle of wine if I could, but you'll have to settle for lemonade. But just so you know, my daughter says I make the best lemonade in the world."

"Well, with Cami's stamp of approval, I'm sure I won't want anything else." Her own words sounded awkward and she shuffled in her seat, pretending to adjust herself to the folding chair.

"We'll see." He opened the lid of a blue cooler and pulled a large glass pitcher from it.

She hadn't seen the cooler that had been behind the folding table, hidden by the linen tablecloth. She ran a finger along the soft fabric, admiring the delicate stitching that had been added to its edges. As she looked up she saw his eyes soften, the lights highlighting their dark color.

"My grandmother. She was an artist with anything to do with stitching. She knitted, cross stitched, you name it. She would have had Cami decked out in her stuff from head to toe." He had finished pouring the lemonade and now he was clearing space in the center of the table.

"I'm sure. This is lovely. I wish I was crafty like that. Aunt Ruby can knit anything and it'll look like it came from a department store. I'm not blessed with talent like that."

He was standing, about to step up away when he stopped. "What are you talking about not being blessed with a talent? Have you heard yourself play?" He walked over to a stack of crates and unsnapped what looked like an over-sized rectangular insulated bag. He slipped on oven mitts and reached in, pulling out a glass casserole dish.

Wide-eyed, Tacy watched him as he placed the dish in the open space on the table. He pulled off the aluminum foil and a ring of steam billowed up in the air, the light catching the way it swirled away.

"What is this?"

"This is my specialty. Now I don't have a lot of specialties, mind you, but Cami said she thinks you'll like this one. This is spaghetti and meatballs baked casserole. I've made it several times and my main critic tells me it's a winner." He took a sip of lemonade and put his glass down.

Tacy thought she saw sweat beading on his forehead. She pushed the thought away. The weather had changed and the night air was cool. And Brody Porter didn't look like the kind of guy who would get nervous over anything.

"It looks fabulous. I'm sure I'll like it." Feeling like she should do something, she reached for a serving spoon only to have Brody reach out and pat her hand gently.

"No, allow me. A chef always serves his creation." He was smiling as he took the spoon and scooped a generous portion of the spaghetti on to her plate, the chunks of melted mozzarella cheese dropping on the linen tablecloth. With a quick move to avoid any further mess, he scooped his own portion and dropped it onto his plate.

"This is so beautiful. You really shouldn't have gone to so much trouble. I was supposed to take you to dinner, remember?" She said it while grinning the whole time. She was beaming inside and out, forgetting what she'd thought about Brody Porter the first time she'd met him.

"I know, but like I said, we don't have too many choices in Hill Top. I know it sounds crazy, but I haven't gone too far from Cami since she was born. I like to stay close to home. And I figured you might not want to leave Ruby for too long either. How's your visit going?"

Tacy took a bite of her food. Cami was right. This was delicious. She was impressed and there was no way to hide it. And she had to admit she liked the way he put his daughter, and even Ruby, first.

"This is delicious. As for my visit, well, it's going fine. I think we're going to be off to a good start tomorrow with the pickers you've found. I really appreciate your help. I think Aunt Ruby's happy that she can help out the preschool." She saw the funny look in his eyes, as if he was waiting for something more.

"Yes, I think you're going to pull off this harvest. I was just wondering how you and Ruby were getting along. I know it's been some time since you've been home."

Tacy filled her mouth with more pasta to buy time. She didn't want to talk about personal things with Brody. After all, he was her aunt's neighbor. Wasn't that chummy enough? And yes they were sharing a candlelit dinner, but it was just dinner.

"Yes, it's been four years, almost five. I've been working hard at my music career. I just don't get time to come home."

"Do you like being back in Hill Top?" He was twirling his spaghetti on his fork.

Her eyes met his and she could see he was just making conversation. She relaxed and took a sip of her lemonade, also quite delicious and something she rarely drank in the city.

"Yes, I have to say I do. Just tonight I was admiring how clear the sky here is. I guess I've forgotten that. It's nice to be able to see the stars without a tower or an antenna blocking your view. Somehow all that stuff just doesn't let you see much of the stars." She took another bite of the delicious pasta, savoring the sauce as she chewed slowly. Home cooked food was something she didn't have often, and when she did, it consisted of pancakes or plain spaghetti, nothing like this. She hadn't realized how hungry she was.

"That's what I like best about Hill Top. I lived in the city before we came here. Once we got settled in here I made it a point to sit out on my porch every night after Cami went to bed and just stare at the sky. Everything looks more beautiful in the glow of the night sky."

She didn't need to look up to know he was staring at her. Her heart pounded against her rib cage and in the silence of the barn she thought she could almost hear it. She couldn't ignore looking at him forever.

Her eyes met his. Was it the heat of the candles making her this warm? Or was it him? She hoped it was the former because she felt she was heading into dangerous territory. The pretty white lights, the glowing candles, good food. It would make any woman think crazy thoughts. But she wasn't a high school girl anymore, like she'd been with Donnie Hays, and thanks to her last failed relationship, she'd learned her lesson. If she thought her heart was racing now, it went into overdrive when he touched her hand.

"Would you like to take a walk through the orchards?"

His large hand covered hers, with a gentle touch. She imagined how safe Cami felt when her father took her hand. Before she could imagine something she shouldn't, she pulled her hand free.

"That's a good idea. The fresh air would be good." The glowing barn was becoming too confining, despite its vastness. She needed a little room to breathe, a little more space between them.

"Great." He pushed his chair away and held out his hand.

Pretending she didn't see it, she stepped away from the table and headed for the darkness outside the open barn doors.

~

It must have been the lights. Brody didn't know what had come over him. Ever since she'd playfully sprayed him earlier in the day, he hadn't been able to think of much else. Cami had tugged at his arm a few times. Apparently she'd been talking to him and he hadn't even heard her. He'd deliberately put his attention on her as she talked about church and showed him the pages she'd colored at Sunday school.

But his mind kept going back to Tacy. He could still see her playing the violin, her eyes closed, a strand of hair falling onto her face. And he hadn't missed the way his daughter had been entranced by the woman. He had to admit there was something about her. He couldn't figure out what to think about her. She was an independent woman and yet it seemed like she was missing something.

Ruby had confided in him during one particular visit to her at the rehabilitation center. Whether she was in particular discomfort that day he didn't know, but he had figured out that the woman had some regrets about her relationship with Tacy. Namely, that she blamed herself for Tacy leaving as abruptly as she had. Which made him wonder if there wasn't something more going on between the two women. Which reminded him that it was none of his business and that the last thing he needed was to get involved with Tacy.

He'd had to remind himself, even as he'd strung those white lights, that she was passing through, only home because he'd made her feel guilty. Once the apples in Ruby's orchard were harvested he had no doubt she would be on her way. She'd said herself she had a very important audition coming up soon. From the look on her face, he could see the passion she had for her music. She wouldn't miss the opportunity.

Now here he was beside her, strolling through the apple trees. He studied her serious face, catching the way her nose turned up as she took in the heady scent of the ripe apples. Between the pale colored dress she wore and the glow of the moonlight, she reminded him of one of the fairy pictures he'd looked at countless times with Cami. The stars blinked above the massive trees, lighting up the dark soft waves of her hair. It looked like she'd dressed especially for their dinner and yet he hadn't missed the way she'd avoided taking his arm. It stung a little and he'd admonished himself in silence. He was making more out of this dinner than it was. After all, she'd probably meant for them to go sit somewhere and eat so they could talk about tomorrow.

"Cami's a wonderful little girl. You seem like a

great dad."

Her words put his train of thoughts that threatened to derail back on track. He gave her a grateful smile.

"Thank you. I don't know about great, but I try my best. She's the love of my life. I just want the best for her. It just seems so unfair for a kid not to have a mother. I mean, especially a girl. A girl needs a mother. I try to be both to her, but I'm guessing someday she's going to notice."

He was sorry he'd gotten so personal. He hadn't talked about that to anyone, not even Ruby. It was better left unsaid. He saw the way her eyes were glistening in the light the night sky was casting on her. He nearly lost his footing when he felt her slip her arm in his.

"I know I haven't been here long, but I'd say you've done a great job. She seems very happy to me. I lost my mom when I was three years old. I barely remember her. Actually, I think I only remember what my uncle and aunt have shared about her with me. And the pictures. There aren't enough to fill an album, but there's enough that I know what she looks like. I never knew my dad, but as I got older I wished I did. At least Cami has one parent that really loves her."

As quick as the words flowed, they stopped. He saw the way her lips clamped tight. He imagined she'd shared more than she'd intended. A weird sensation filled his chest. He wanted to soothe the heartbroken child he saw in her the way he did when Cami came to him in tears on occasion after a spat at preschool. Instead, he pulled her close to him and kissed her on the lips.

As their lips met and he closed his eyes, everything seemed to spin, the light of the stars flashing on the leaves. He held on to her tight. She didn't pull away. When he had left the warmth of her mouth he opened his eyes. Her lashes glimmered and he touched her cheek. He had guessed right. He wiped at the tear that trickled from her eye.

"Are you okay?" The words came out on his breath. It was the first thing he thought of. She stayed in his arms for a moment and then he felt her inch out of his arms.

"I'm…I'm fine." She stammered.

They stood there among the trees, under the moonlit starry sky just staring at each other, neither looking sure of what to do next. Tacy made the first move.

"Maybe we should clean up the barn now. I've got a long day ahead of me tomorrow." And with her lead, he followed her back through the trees up to the barn that glowed in the distance. He could have kicked himself, but it was too late. The damage was done.

## Chapter Eleven

There had been no time for Tacy to mull over what happened the night before. No time to replay the kiss that had almost knocked her off her heels. Since she'd been expecting Jack, Erin and Mary Ellen, her picking crew, she'd gotten up early to be ready for the day. She told herself the mammoth butterflies hitting her stomach wall were the result of nerves over the day ahead, not the occasional thought about that kiss that she'd pushed to the back of her mind.

It was a little after six. She wasn't sure if Aunt Ruby would remember that she'd told her she'd be heading out to the barn by seven the next morning. She'd decided to shower and dress as quiet as she could and then cook up a breakfast that her aunt could reheat when she woke up later on.

The frying pan sizzled as she poured the whipped eggs in. With a whisk she scrambled the four eggs as she watched the toaster oven on the counter. She would leave a bowl of scrambled eggs in the refrigerator with the strawberries she'd found with a sticky note that said, in childish scribble, 'Grammy Ruby'.

She'd nearly lost her thought after seeing that label. She had wracked her memory, but couldn't remember hearing Cami call her aunt that since she'd gotten there. It distracted her enough to forget what she'd gone in the refrigerator for. She had pulled herself together and took out the container of orange juice.

Standing at the counter, she rushed through her scrambled eggs in between intermittent bites of buttered toast. She guzzled her orange juice and dropped her plate and glass in the sink. About to walk away, she thought twice and turned on the water. With hurried moves, she washed and rinsed both and left them in the dish rack. It was one less thing her aunt would feel inclined to do herself. She left the kitchen and headed out to the living room.

Glancing around and seeing everything in order, she was satisfied that all her aunt would have to do would be to warm her breakfast and get herself to the living room. She even made sure the night before that her knitting would be in reach by the chair her aunt liked to knit in. She stared at the clock on the wooden side table. It was only six forty. She'd told Brody to have the teens meet her at the barn by seven. It would probably be best if she got there before them in order to open up the barn and have things ready.

She stood rooted to the living room floor, debating on whether she should check in on her aunt or just leave. She tiptoed down the hall and listened outside her aunt's door. No sound came from the room. She was probably still sleeping. Tacy decided to let her rest and leave. She'd posted her cell phone number all over the house so that if her aunt needed anything she could reach Tacy right away.

She inhaled the crisp morning air and rubbed her arms. She'd decided to wear an old pair of coveralls she'd found at the back of her closet with an old t-shirt that she wouldn't mind should it get worse for the wear today. For a moment she thought about grabbing her sweatshirt then decided against it. Feeling for her cell phone in the side pocket of her coveralls, she took long strides towards the path to the barn and orchards.

Within minutes she was in front of the barn. She stared at it as if it were unrecognizable. Any traces of the transformation that had occurred there last night were gone. In the light of day, the barn looked like any other barn instead of like the magical place it had been for a few short hours the night before. She almost felt like Cinderella after her carriage had changed back into a pumpkin.

Eager to get started, she struggled slightly to open the doors. The early morning sunlight flooded the barn. She walked over to the tractor and wagon that Brody had helped attach last night. Inside the wagon were dozens of apple baskets all clean and dry, ready to go. The aprons they had inspected for rips and holes were also piled neatly on the crates behind the wagon waiting for a much larger crew than she was expecting.

Her heart froze for a moment. Just how much could a team of three people really pick? She knew from experience that her uncle never had less than twelve apple pickers during the times when he was depending on a certain amount of apples for sale. The majority of the harvest went to local stands and the rest to the church.

Somehow now it seemed more urgent than before that the orchard reap enough apples for the church. This time the preschool was depending on it. She didn't want to let the church preschool down. *Or Brody Porter.*

She pushed any thought of Brody out of her mind and climbed inside the tractor. Uncle Jerry had always had the tractor outside of the barn ready for the picking crew. After the crew suited up their aprons, he would drive the baskets out and put them within the rows so each picker had access to them. Each time a picker's apron would fill to the brim, they'd walk over to the basket and carefully roll their apples into it, freeing their apron for the next batch they picked.

Sitting high up on her uncle's tractor felt good. It surprised her how much she enjoyed driving the old thing. But then she'd counted down the days until her uncle had deemed her old enough to drive it. Now here she was in charge. Odd how that made her feel. She positioned the tractor along the side of the barn, ready to drive it out to her crew, one of which would be her. She left the tractor and walked back inside the barn to pile up the ladders next to the crate. If each picker could carry their own ladder out that would be a great help.

Seeing the crew was so small, she thought maybe she'd follow after the three teens with the tractor so the baskets would be out there. She was surprised to find herself looking forward to a challenge like this. It had absolutely nothing to do with music and getting a spot in the orchestra.

"Anybody here?" A young girl's voice called out.

Tacy turned around to see a tall, thin girl with long brown hair peering at her.

"Hi! I'm Tacy. Are you Mary Ellen or Erin?" She walked over and stuck her hand out. The girl took her hand and squeezed it. As she pulled it away, Tacy noticed the clunky school ring with a blue stone in the center.

"I'm Erin. Mary Ellen should be coming along with Jack any minute. Jack had to help out for a little while at his family's deli, so Mary Ellen was waiting there to come with him."

"That's great. I really appreciate you guys being willing to help. I'm not sure what Brody told you or if you've ever picked apples before."

Erin smiled and shook her head.

"Not like a job, but when we were little my family always went apple picking. I'm a fast learner so I'm sure I'll be fine." She tucked one hand in her jeans pocket and looked around.

Tacy hesitated, unsure of whether she should mention anything about money. She was sure kids their ages were interested in making a little money. They could be home sleeping during this week of no classes that only came once a year. It was an effort to come out this early. She had to offer them something.

"I don't know if Brody told you anything more than it was just a few days of picking. I can only give you each twenty dollars a day for the days you pick, if that's okay. I know it should be more, but I'm kind of low on cash myself right now, and my aunt isn't able to pay anyone." The girl held up her hand and nodded her head.

"Oh, no, don't worry about that. We already made a deal with Brody." She was twirling her hair with the finger that sported the clunky school ring and looking around the barn.

"Deal? What kind of deal?"

"He said if we do this for him, he'll give us all the drinks we want and free samples for the rest of the school year." The girl turned a bright pink, as if she knew she'd said something maybe she should have kept to herself.

"We really didn't expect anything. We would have helped for free. He's the one that offered. He knows we've been looking for jobs and I guess he thought he'd help us out. He's a good guy like that, you know?"

Still in shock, Tacy nodded her head while in her mind she calculated just how much Brody Porter would have to pay to get her aunt's orchards picked. The indignation she'd felt just a few days ago after finding out he'd tricked her into coming home for his own benefit was quickly being replaced by something else. He'd more than made up for what he'd done with a dinner of hotdogs, getting her car back to the house and that dinner last night. Was this how far he would go just to make sure his daughter's preschool had funding for the year? She was impressed to say the least. Before she could say anything, a boy and girl the same age as Erin came walking up to them.

"You're Jack and Mary Ellen, right?" She stuck out a hand to one at a time and they took it, giving it a friendly shake. They quickly stood beside Erin.

"So, I guess you guys are my crew. At least for today. I'm still trying to get additional pickers for tomorrow, but I've found it's tougher than it used to be. To get started, you can each strap on an apron and grab a ladder. If you can manage the ladders, you all will walk out to the beginning of the orchard and I'll follow you with the tractor and baskets. It's early enough that we should be able to make some progress and then break for lunch. I'll head up to the house and have pizzas delivered for you guys. After that we'll go as long as we have daylight, but if you have to leave earlier I understand. If you have any questions, feel free to ask away and…"

A familiar woman's voice broke into her spiel. She turned to see Lucy Aimes-Hurley and two young men whom she had to do a double take before she realized they were her brothers.

"I heard you were hiring." A huge grin spread from ear to ear on Lucy's face.

"Lucy? Michael and Peter?" She dropped more than the aprons as she hurried over and wrapped her arms around her long lost friend.

~

No matter how busy he tried to keep himself, Brody couldn't stop thinking about Tacy. Or the kiss they had shared. He'd replayed the scene over and and over in his mind, each time analyzing a different detail, looking for something he might have missed the time before. She had let him kiss her. She'd stay in his arms. She'd kissed him back. Of that he was sure. As he stood waiting for the whirring machine to stop, he touched his mouth, as if he might be able to feel a trace of her lips on his, feel the warmth that had stayed with him even hours after she'd pulled away and started for the barn. He was sure she'd enjoyed it, even wanted it to happen. That tear he'd wiped away, he was sure had nothing to do with him. It didn't seem like the moment to ask her to dig in to her heart and share what was bothering her. But he was sure it wasn't him or that kiss. More likely it had something to do with a childhood wound that hadn't healed. He'd suspected she and Ruby had something between them that had gone unsaid. It wasn't his place to get involved. He had no business even kissing her. He'd gotten as far off course from his vow to himself as he possibly could. He was angry with himself and yet when he pictured Tacy talking to Cami about playing the violin he wanted to excuse himself. Tacy Clark had found the only way his heart could possibly ever open - through his daughter.

He looked up from the counter to the lone small round table directly to the side of the counter, the one reserved for employees, namely he and Lucy, to sit down for a coffee break. Cami's blond curls had spilled onto her face in her deep concentration as she colored in the coloring book she'd had in her hands as she'd run out of the school doors that morning. Twelve o'clock always seemed to come so fast and usually when he was in the thick of things. Luckily today, a day when he had sacrificed Lucy's help, the shop had been empty around noon. He'd taken the opportunity to lock the doors and run out to pick Cami up, knowing they'd be back within fifteen minutes. He'd turned the 'be back soon' sign on the door and taken off.

Now his little girl was sitting happily at the table coloring, a chocolate chip cookie half eaten on a napkin at her elbow. He was grateful she wasn't the type of child who needed to be on the run for hours at a time. It was close to five o'clock now and he'd caught all the late afternoon caffeine seeking customers he usually did. For some reason the day just seemed to drag on, despite the brisk business he'd done all day long. Now he was eager to pack up and take Cami home.

He thought about the next day and wondered if he'd reminded Lucy that he would need her for opening.

Lizzy Hart had an early morning dental appointment and so he wouldn't be able to drop Cami off as early as he'd need to. Staring at his cell phone on the counter, he thought about giving her a quick call to be sure. But she was probably still in the orchards, knee deep in apples, and who knew if she'd hear her phone ring?

"Cami, get your crayons and coloring book put in your backpack. We're going home now." He untied his apron, dropped his phone in his back pocket and headed to the back room. The ovens had been off for hours, the room finally cool. Pans and trays lay soaking in a sink full of suds. He didn't want to leave that mess for Lucy. If he could make some arrangements for Cami in the morning, he could come in early and clean it up before she found it. He flipped the switches and the small kitchen was dark with the exception of a ray of light coming in from the small window on the wall opposite the ovens.

"Cami? Are you ready?" He watched his daughter as she strategically placed each crayon in her pouch, then dropped the coloring book into her pink backpack.

"Yup. Where are we going, Daddy?" She stood alongside him, her little head angled up so her eyes could meet his. The curly locks of blond hair fell every which way as she stared at him.

"Home, honey. It's time to go home." He put a hand gently on the top of her head and guided her to the door. They stepped outside into the crisp fall air. She waited at his side as he turned the key in the lock and pulled on the door to be sure.

"Home to Ruby and Tacy or home to our house?" She was peering up at him, her bright blue eyes squinting against the late day sun, her eyebrows scrunched together questioningly.

Brody scratched at his beard, thrown off by the unexpected question. He bent down and picked her up, settling her on his right hip. "Sweetie, you know home is our house." He wanted to leave it at that. He headed for his pickup and lowered her to the curb, opening the door so she could climb in. She flung her backpack to the back seat.

"I know, but I like living at Grammy Ruby's house."

Brody's eyes widened. This was the first he'd heard her call Ruby Grammy. He'd puzzled over what his daughter should call the woman after their friendship began to cement. Ruby had taken a shine to Cami from the very first day. Calling her Mrs. Clark had seemed too formal, too stiff. Before he could obsess any further over it, Ruby herself had told him it would be fine if the little girl wanted to call her by her first name. This was the first he'd heard of 'Grammy'.

"Grammy Ruby? When did you start calling her that?"

"A while ago, when Tacy came. Ruby said it seemed like a good idea. I like having a Grammy. All the other girls at school have a Grammy." Her bottom lip jut out as she folded her arms across her tiny body.

Her last words nearly ripped his heart apart. Another reminder of how he had failed to give her a family, a real family. If Carrie Ann, Cami's mother, had stayed would they have Saturday night pizza parties with her mother? Would Cami call Carrie Ann's mother Grammy? Remembering that he'd only met his estranged wife's mother a few times, he figured not.

The woman looked about as cuddly as a lizard.

Feeling defeated, he just reached over and pushed the hair from her face.

"Then that's what you should call her." He wasn't going to argue who was family and who wasn't with his four year old daughter. She was right of course. All the other little girls at school probably did have a Grammy. It broke his heart not only that she didn't have one, but the fact that she knew it too.

"Can we go there now?" She was looking at him with a hopeful smile.

"Where?"

Looking exasperated with him, she rolled her baby blues.

"To Grammy Ruby's house. I want to show her the new coloring book that Miss Lizzy gave me at school today."

He turned the ignition and pulled away from the curb, checking out the window and hoping that she'd see he was too busy to answer.

"So can we? Can we now?"

It was no use. He knew his daughter too well. When she wanted to do something or go somewhere they had a routine. She persisted and he gave in.

"Okay, we can. I have to talk to Miss Lucy anyway and make sure she knows she has to open up tomorrow." He watched her pull her legs up underneath her and adjust herself so she could see the scenery as they made their way down Main Street. A happy, satisfied look came over her face.

Dad = 0 Cami = 1. The usual score. As they drove through the business district and on to the dirt road where they'd stopped paving Main Street, Brody took in the beginnings of the change in color all around them. With his daughter happily gazing out the passenger window, he felt happier than he had in a long time. He felt a flutter inside he couldn't quite name. It was probably just the first time he'd stopped to realize just how good his life in Hill Top was. It had nothing to do with the fact that they were heading to Ruby's house and the orchards where Tacy and her crew were working. Or the fact that he would have to ride over to the orchards to catch up with Lucy. And run into Tacy as he did so. No, it's just that his life was coming together better than he'd thought it could have.

He turned down the long dirt driveway that led to Ruby's farmhouse. Out of the corner of his eye he saw his daughter pull herself up in excitement. He hesitated in front of the house before shutting off the ignition, debating on whether to leave Cami with Ruby for a few minutes or drive themselves straight to the orchards.

"Sweetie, Miss Lucy is in the orchards with Miss Tacy…"

"Can I go see Miss Tacy too?" Hands clapping, she was bobbing up and down in her seat.

"Honey, I'm not going to see Miss Tacy. I'm going to see Miss Lucy about the coffee shop." He almost had to bite his tongue to keep from smiling. It looked like he wasn't the only one who wouldn't mind seeing Miss Tacy again.

"Yes you are. You like Miss Tacy. You had dinner with her yesterday and everything."

He had to wonder what constituted everything in a four year old's world, but didn't ask. He wasn't sure he wanted to hear the answer.

"Cami, Miss Tacy is very nice and yes we had dinner, but that's because Miss Tacy is helping the church raise money for your preschool."

She shook her head vigorously, her blond curls bobbing back and forth, refusing to accept what he said.

"Do you understand? Miss Tacy is a friend and she's helping us because we are her friends." He watched her shake her head again, this time her lips pursed, an irritated look in her eyes.

He gave up. He turned the truck towards the dirt path he'd almost pulled his back out for as he cleared the bramble and vines from and drove slowly towards the barn.

As they drew closer to the barn he recognized the lone small blue car that was Lucy Aimes-Hurley's. His eyes scanned the open barn for Lucy, Jack, Erin or Mary Ellen. He spotted a tall lean girl and figured it was Erin. He parked in front of the fence on the right side of the barn, as far from the doors as possible to allow the tractor to have as much birth as possible to get in the barn. He shut the truck off, but before he could say another word Cami jumped out and ran along the back of his truck, heading straight for the barn.

He closed his truck door and peered in to the barn, his eyes looking for Tacy. His eyes took in Lucy and her two brothers as they sipped from cans of soda in their hands. Sure enough he saw Erin standing in a huddle with Jack and Mary Ellen West, the three teens alternating between laughing and drinking from cans as well.

For a moment he wondered if Tacy had left the crew to themselves to do something else. He thought about her Beetle that she had mentioned needing to take a town over for repairs. He couldn't imagine her leaving everything to her inexperienced crew on the very first day. Maybe she was already back at the farmhouse, making Ruby dinner.

He chided himself for feeling disappointed after riding so high the whole trip here. Just as he was about to approach Lucy and her brothers, he caught site of her coming from a stall in the barn. He stopped short and stared at her. As if she could feel his eyes on her, she looked up. The fleeting smile she gave him was so quick he had to convince himself he actually saw one. He gave her a wave to which she waved back. When he saw her disappear back into the stall, he pulled himself together and approached Lucy. That was the whole reason he'd come to the barn to begin with, wasn't it?

"Hey, Lucy. Hey Michael, Peter. How did your day go?" It had been his idea talking Lucy into giving Tacy a hand. He admitted to himself it had more to do with getting apples picked. He'd seen the look crossing between the two women's eyes that day in Evie's Cafe. How silly for these two not to talk to one another after being the best of friends for so many years?

"Good. It went pretty well considering between us we've never picked like that before. But we pulled a good haul. I think Tacy was very happy." Lucy was beaming as she spoke, occasionally glancing in the direction of the stall Tacy had disappeared into.

Michael and Peter shook the hand he extended and walked over to the group of teens he'd recruited from the coffee shop.

Brody's eyes followed Lucy's, but Tacy was out of sight. He turned his attention back to Lucy.

"I wanted to be sure you knew that I needed you

to open tomorrow. Lizzy Hart has that dental appointment, so I'll have Cami until nine when preschool starts."

Lucy had cocked her head sideways and was staring at him over her soda can.

"You came all the way here to remind me? You could have just called my cell. I'd had it in my pocket the whole day." She was grinning at him.

"Yes, well I wasn't sure if you'd get a signal out here and I didn't want to take a chance. And it's no problem since I live one house over from here anyway. And Cami wanted to see Miss Ruby." He craned his neck, searching the barn for Cami. Where did she go anyway? Lucy touched his arm.

"Don't worry. She's fine. She zig zagged in here like a bolt of lightning and headed straight to Tacy. She's helping Tacy with the crates for the apples."

Brody didn't like the way Lucy was grinning at him. He was asking about his daughter. What was so funny about that?

"Oh, sure. I had a feeling she was somewhere around here..." His words died on his lips.

"Brody, you can't fool me. I know you too well. We've worked together every day for almost three years now. You didn't come all the way down here just to make sure I didn't forget tomorrow, which I told you the other day I had marked on my calendar at home." She pretended to be insulted, but couldn't hold back a giggle.

"I'm sorry if I insulted you. I know you never let me down. But I did come here just for that." He bit his lip. The last thing he needed was Lucy telling people that he was falling for Tacy. He didn't need Ruby hearing it. He didn't need Cami hearing it, what with her little imagination already making up stories, and he sure didn't need Tacy hearing it. He shifted his weight from left to right, feeling uncomfortable under Lucy's scrutinizing looks.

"I've got to get Cami home. She needs dinner and her bath. Would you do me a favor, and go get her and send her out to my truck? I'd like to get going." With that he turned around and walked out of the barn.

He walked past Lucy's small car and jumped into his pickup truck. Tapping his thumb against the steering wheel he watched for Cami at the opening of the barn. His heart nearly jumped out of his chest when he saw Tacy holding her hand as she walked her out. As she watched Cami sprint to the truck, she looked up at him and their eyes met. She gave him a quick nod, turned around and disappeared back into the barn.

Cami threw the door open and jumped in. Without a word, he turned the truck on, backed up and headed for the opening at the other end of the path that led to the road back to his own home. He glanced in the rear view mirror but no one stood in the opening of the barn doors. Good. It was just as well. It was time to stick to his original promise to himself and get back on track. In a few days the apples would be picked and Tacy Clark would be on her way back to her life and he could get on with his.

But as he pulled into the driveway of his fixer upper Dutch colonial, he couldn't help notice that it seemed darker than usual for this time of day.

# Chapter Twelve

The long busy day of picking apples had been a welcome respite for Tacy. They'd cleaned up the barn as a team and, one by one, her picking crew had left her with no choice but to go home. It was Tuesday, and Sunday seemed like worlds ago, when she'd last saw Brody. She had to keep telling herself it was for the best, but it felt like her heart physically ached every time she walked the dirt path he'd cleared for her. During clean up, she'd decided that she hadn't spent enough time with her aunt. Sure, she was doing what needed to be done. She had arranged to get the barn ready for a picking crew, regardless of how small it was. She tried to forget that without Brody Porter there would be no crew.

She grabbed her shoulder length hair and wrapped an elastic around it as she prepared dinner for herself and Ruby. She'd been wanting to practice her cooking skills and this night was the perfect chance. She was making a beef and broccoli Chinese dish that she'd only made once before. She was sure it was something her aunt would enjoy. With her crew busy at work earlier in the day, she'd asked Lucy's brother Michael if she could borrow his car to run to Dunley's Mini Mart. She had run up and down the aisles grabbing everything she'd need to make the dish. She'd tossed the meat and fresh broccoli in the refrigerator and the rest of the ingredients on the counter and shot back out to the orchards with only a wave to her aunt.

Now sizzling sounds from the frying pan and a delicious soy scent wafted in the air. She had to admit it smelled pretty good. She'd settled Ruby in to her favorite chair with her knitting while she cooked. She left the stove for a moment to take a peek at her and see if she was okay. Her aunt looked up from her knitting and smiled at her.

"So, are Cami and Brody coming to join us for dinner?"

Tacy tried not to let her aunt see how much the question upset her.

"No, not tonight. I thought it would be nice if I spent some time just with you. It seems like I've been so busy getting ready for the festival that I've barely spent any time with you. Tonight it's just you and me." She saw her aunt smile and then go to get up. She ran over to help her.

"Can I get you something, Aunt Ruby?" She'd rather get whatever it was for her so her aunt could rest. She'd thought she'd heard her groan a few times over the last day or so, unusual because on Sunday she'd thought she seemed well on her way to mending. The thought disappointed her. She didn't intend to stay too much longer. The annual harvest festival was four days away. She'd figured at that point her aunt would be doing well enough for her to leave. She needed the next week or two to prepare for the audition.

"Well, yes, dear if you wouldn't mind going into the hall linen closet. On the bottom shelf you'll see a few albums. If you could get me the album with the rose print maybe..." Her words followed Tacy as she raced for the closet. She threw it open and scanned the shelves. There on the bottom shelf were three or four albums, all blue with the exception of the album her aunt had asked for. She grabbed it, closed the door and headed back to the living room.

"Is this the right one?" She laid the album gently in her aunt's lap. Her aunt's eyes lit up so she guessed it was.

"I'm going to check on dinner. We should be eating in five minutes or less." Seeing her aunt engrossed in pictures as she flipped the pages of the album, Tacy left her to check the stove. As she had guessed, the food was ready. She'd already set the table for two, thinking it would be easier to eat in the kitchen versus the dining room. And she wouldn't be picturing Brody at the dining room table as they eat their food.

"We're all ready. Let me help you with your walker." She took the album from her aunt and laid it on the side table beside the chair. She wheeled the walker over to her and made sure her aunt had a firm grasp before they started for the kitchen.

"Tacy, this smells wonderful! What a treat!" Her aunt accepted the chair Tacy held out for her.

Tacy took the bowl with the beef and broccoli and placed it in the center of the table alongside a bowl of brown rice she'd made to go with it. She spooned out generous portions of both on to her aunt's plate. Steam whirled above their plates as they waited to take a bite.

"I hope you like it. I've only made it once before, but it turned out pretty good. I think your kitchen is more equipped to experiment with recipes than the closet of a kitchen I have back in the city." She saw her aunt smile and nod as she scooped a forkful of the beef and broccoli. She pushed a forkful of the same in her own mouth. She was right. The right kitchen made all the difference. During the last year or two she'd surprised herself as she found out how much she enjoyed cooking different foods. Unfortunately, her budget didn't allow for her to buy the things she wanted to try too often.

"It's delicious. It tastes as good as it smells. Thank you."

For the rest of the evening they ate in between occasional chatter. Her aunt asked her about her music and she asked her aunt about the goings on in town since she'd left. She found it oddly comforting how little life in Hill Top had changed.

After she'd convinced her aunt to let the pan and plates soak in the sink, they moved back to the living room. It was then that Tacy really took note of the album she had gotten for her aunt earlier. The name across the top of the album caught her eye first. Ruby Henderson.

"I didn't know your name was Henderson before it was Clark. But if Uncle Jerry was Clark, then how did I get his last name and not my...my mother's? Wasn't she Henderson too?" She hadn't asked her aunt about her mother in a very long time. When she was younger her aunt's reaction hadn't been very good. After that, she'd let it go. Uncle Jerry had been the one to share details of her mother's life and her infancy. This name thing puzzled her.

Ruby shook her head, a sad look in her eyes.

"Yes, your mother, my sister, was a Henderson too. But when...when she found out you were coming along she asked Jerry if he would be okay with giving you his name. So you were Tacy Clark right from the start."

Tacy still didn't understand.

"But...but what about my father? Uncle Jerry said his name was Severo. Severo Gonzalez, right?"

"Yes, it was, but he left before you were born. By that point, Fern, your mother, knew she wanted something stable for her baby girl. She gave you our name, my name by marriage. Your Uncle Jerry always considered you a Clark."

Tacy thought about this startling revelation. All these years she'd wondered how she had the same name as her aunt and uncle. He had never shared this story with her. She looked down at the pictures her aunt was gently fingering in the album.

"Is that my mom?" Tacy stared at the sunny blond haired teenager in the picture. "How old was she then?" She couldn't take her eyes off of Fern Henderson even to look at her aunt as she spoke.

"Oh, that was just around the time she'd graduated high school. She was about ready to go to college." She stopped speaking for a moment, wiped at her eye and continued.

"But she put it off. She said she wanted to follow her dreams. She had big dreams, my sister. She loved to sing. I swear that's where you got your musical talent from. She would come and go here and there as she found gigs, as she called them. She'd go from band to band. Then one time she'd decided to come back here and go to school. She even thought she'd take voice and drama classes. She did well. She was in school about three years, so close to finishing. Then she met....your father. And she found herself pregnant at twenty three and unmarried. She refused to tell us who the father was, but your uncle had seen the way she and Severo had looked at each other. We figured as much. She was such a dreamer. She thought she could do anything, even have a baby and continue her music. But she dropped out of school." Her aunt stopped speaking and felt along the side table for the box of tissues. Tacy grabbed the box and handed them to her. Her aunt blew her nose and looked up at Tacy.

"I shouldn't be going on about this. What's done is done. I...it still upsets me to this day."

Tacy patted her hand and pointed to another picture.

"I hate to see you upset, Aunt Ruby, but I'd really like to know more." She wanted to push her to tell her everything. To spill every last detail of the life she'd only had vague pieces of the puzzle to for all these years.

"You're right. You should know. You haven't got much of your history. I regret not sharing more with you but it was just so hard. She was my sister. My baby sister." As if she were on a mission, her aunt straightened herself up and put the tissue down.

"When you were about three years old, your mother had gone out for the night. She loved to go out at night. She never worried. She knew you were safe with your uncle and me. That night there was a terrible rainstorm. The roads were flooding and because there was still some ice from an early frost, they were slick. We had a feeling she was with him. Your father. Your uncle waited up until the early morning hours for her. Instead, a policeman came to the door to tell us there had been an accident. They were gone." She stopped, too emotional to continue and reached for the tissue again. Tacy grabbed a tissue and dabbed at her own eyes, overcome by the tragedy she was only just learning about.

"They? That was the accident that killed my mother?" She waited, heart in her mouth, for the answer she feared was coming. All the fantasies she'd entertained herself with during her early teens, the stories she'd imagined of her father coming to tell her he loved her and had been looking for her for years, seemed about to burst like a fragile soap bubble, the sting burning her eyes.

"Not just your mother, dear. Your father too. They died together in that accident." Her aunt wept in silence, trying her best not to upset Tacy anymore than she must have seen she had.

Tacy was blinded by her unexpected tears. She wiped at her runny nose that threatened to soak her lips. She sank down on the sofa opposite her aunt and stared at her in disbelief.

"Why didn't you tell me before today? All these years I hung on to the idea that maybe he was out there. That he would come and look for me one day. It kept me going all those days when I knew you didn't want me here." She saw her aunt jolt upright in her seat.

"Didn't want you here? Where on earth did you get that idea?" Tear filled, reddened eyes met hers.

More tears threatened to spill over. Tacy took a deep breath and looked her aunt in the eyes, fighting to hold back the tears.

"I heard you. I heard you tell Uncle Jerry. I knew it was wrong, but I was listening outside your bedroom door when I was nine years old. I heard you say you had never planned to have children. That you couldn't do it." The words tumbled out of her mouth one after the other. She felt spent. They'd been weighing on her all these years and now they were said. It was out in the open. She'd long suspected it was the reason why she'd never felt close to her aunt. Why she'd been so attached to her uncle, so needy.

Now her aunt was clutching her walker as she made her way over to the sofa where Tacy was seated.

"Oh, Tacy, no. You did hear me say those words, but you left before you heard the rest. Yes, I had never planned to have children. Yes, I said I couldn't do it. I never felt I would make a good mother. Never had that urge. Then you came along. When my sister would hand you over to me, my heart beat in a way it had never done before. And that night your uncle was asking me if I wanted to have a child of my own and I told him I already had. You. I told him I could never want for a child because I already had what I needed in you." As the words escaped her lips in between tiny cries, Aunt Ruby wrapped her arms around her.

And Tacy let herself fall into her aunt's arms and sob deep loud cries. And in that moment Tacy felt like she'd come home. In that moment she'd decided to stay in Hill Top with Aunt Ruby.

Then an image of Brody Porter crossed her mind and the words he'd said that night in the barn. 'She's the love of my life' and she knew she couldn't. Staying with Aunt Ruby would mean having to see Brody Porter and in that moment she knew it would be just too painful to see a man every day that she already knew she was falling for.

Sobbing harder with the realization, she stayed enveloped in her aunt's arms and let her aunt console her broken heart.

~

Brody laid out a rather unusual feast on the dining room table. The hodge-podge of Cami's favorite foods would have been something he reserved for a Friday night as opposed to a Tuesday dinner. But in his head he kept hearing his daughter saying she liked 'staying' at Grammy Ruby's house. Having had his daughter's heart all to himself since she was an infant, he felt foolish. As if he was competing for her love with someone else.

After analyzing his daughter's words while he showered, it finally dawned on him that it wasn't Ruby who made him feel threatened. It was Tacy. He hadn't counted on anything like this happening. He had only wanted to talk Tacy into coming home to get the orchard picked. All he wanted was to see that the church preschool got the funds it needed to offer full day classes for the next year. He'd never even considered that his little girl would take a shine to Ruby's niece. Even worse, he'd never intended to either.

"Yum!" Cami circled the rectangular table that he'd picked up at a thrift shop when they'd first moved to Hill Top. For twenty-five dollars he'd gotten a great deal, despite the weeks it had taken to clean it up. After sanding and repairing and finally painting the table, it looked like it had come from an expensive furniture store.

She stopped at a plate of alphabet shaped chicken fingers, her sunny curls out of her face with the help of a fuchsia color headband she'd proudly put on by herself earlier that day. She looked up at him with a crooked smile.

"I can eat anything here I want? I can pick out my own stuff?" A look that was a cross between glee and doubt was in her eyes.

"Yup. Tonight we're having a daddy daughter feast! I made all of your favorites and you pick out whatever you want to eat tonight."

He stroked the top of her head, the soft cotton-like feel of her hair a contrast to his own callused palms. It made him laugh. How many baristas had callouses? Of course his had nothing to do with his work. It was his passion that shaped his hands. All the projects around this fixer upper that he'd worked on during the two plus years they'd been in town. Whenever he had the time he was either refinishing a piece of thrift shop furniture, repairing walls in the upstairs bedrooms or working on the playhouse he'd promised Cami. As he looked around the room he couldn't help but feel proud. The dining room in particular had come a long way. The walls had shown signs of water damage, the molding had been cracked and missing in places and the floors were worn so badly that there were dips throughout the room.

After he had cleaned up and repaired the rooms, he'd begun to looking for furniture to fill it with. He'd even found six high back chairs to go around the table. After he'd stained them to match the table, he'd thought about how foolish he was. It was only he and Cami. Between the coffee shop and taking care of his daughter he hadn't had time to entertain. And who would he entertain? He thought of Lucy but inviting her and her husband would make him a third wheel.

The tug of Cami's hand on his shirt got his attention.

"Yes, honey?"

"And I can have alphabet chicken, macaroni and cheese, and bologna?" She was grinning wide at him now, her little hand already clasped around three alphabet letters made of chicken.

"Yes, you can. But this is a special occasion. We can't do this all the time. Just for today."

She was such a smart little girl. Even as she scooped spoonfuls of macaroni and cheese on to her plate, he saw her watching him out of the corner of her eye. He knew it was only a matter of time until she questioned him again.

As her hand rolled up a slice of bologna, his thoughts went back to Tacy. He'd busied himself all day long with the coffee shop, attending to customers, checking on croissants and pastries in the ovens, and just plain making small talk with anyone and everyone. He hadn't missed the funny look Lucy had shot him as he chattered from customer to customer, himself feeling like the words were coming out rapid fire from his mouth. He'd thought he'd been doing all right until he'd gotten to Dunley's Mini Mart.

He'd had a list of items needed for Brews & Bites. Though he got a lot of supplies shipped in bulk every two weeks, there was always something little that he tended to run out of. Usually he sent Lucy out while he manned the shop. Today he'd felt like getting out and getting a change of scenery. So he'd run the errand himself. The look in Lucy's eyes told him she was wondering what was up. He shot out the door before she could ask.

He'd been enjoying wheeling his cart up and down the aisles. Even though it was a business trip, he hadn't failed to find one or two things he thought Cami would enjoy and he threw them in his cart. He had chatted with familiar faces and tooted new treats that would be coming to the shop very soon. He had been so involved in his mission that the only thing on his mind was getting a half dozen tubs of butter. Until he had found himself in front of the deli.

Figuring he'd surprise Cami with her favorite, bologna, he had wheeled his cart into the line and waited his turn. His ears had perked up when he heard a woman's voice ordering low sodium ham. Tacy Clark was at the top of the deli line. For a moment he had been frozen to the floor, unable to move left or right. He stared at her profile, her dark locks framing her face as her hands explained how thin she needed the ham cut. He took in the soft green sweater and black leggings with boots she was wearing. The heat surrounded him and he swiped at his forehead.

As she reached for her package of deli meat, he had angled himself behind the big burly man in front of him, hoping he was out of view. As her cart had wheeled away from the deli he let out his breath, waiting for his heart to stop pounding.

He felt his pulse quicken just thinking about it now. He was acting like a school boy instead of a forty year old father.

He grabbed a plate and mindlessly tossed a few alphabet chicken nuggets on his plate, followed by a scoop of macaroni and cheese. He skipped the bologna and pulled out a chair next to his daughter.

"Good?" He asked. He bit into the nugget and

was surprised that it tasted pretty good. It wasn't the nutritious meal he always tried to provide, but she sure looked happy. And hopefully had forgotten all about wanting to see Ruby and Tacy. She swallowed a mouthful and looked at him.

"Yup. I'm going have more. Aren't you going to eat some bologna? It's the best." A small finger pointed to an empty spot on his plate.

"Oh, sure. I'll have some later on. I just wanted to try these nuggets first. They're pretty good." He noshed on another nugget and reached into the bowl of potato chips he'd put out. Potato chips at dinner. He was really losing it.

"Can you color with me in my new book from Miss Lizzy? She even gave me some more crayons to color with. Can you?" Bright blue eyes pleaded with him. She was probably already thinking about her impending bed time.

Cami tried her best each night to stay up late. He'd been trying since she was a toddler to get her used to going to bed at seven every night. Unfortunately, as a single father a lot of nights didn't go as planned and by the time they got home from the coffee shop it was after six and he still had to make dinner. It was just another reminder that if she had a mom at home she wouldn't have to traipse back and forth from preschool to the coffee shop all day. And she would have been able to eat an early dinner and spend that time at six o'clock when he came in the door doing something fun instead of helping speed things up in the kitchen.

He pushed the thought from his mind and focused on the little face staring up at him.

"Of course. You can show me all the new colors

Miss Lizzy gave you and we'll pick out a special picture to color together."

Satisfied with his answer, she dug her fork into the macaroni and cheese stuffed her mouth. He joined her and for a few minutes they chewed in silence. Suddenly she pushed off her chair and stood up.

"Are you all done? Sure you don't want something else?"

She shook her head, blond curls fighting to escape from the confines of the bright fuchsia headband.

"Nope. I'm done. Let's color." She scurried to the hall where she dropped her backpack each day after school.

Brody pushed his chair out and followed. Perched like a tiny bird on the living room floor, her back pack unzipped beside her, the coloring book and crayons were sprawled across the carpet. Brody grinned and lowered himself to the floor, sure he heard his knees crack as he did.

Now this was nice. He couldn't remember the last time the two of them just spent an evening having fun without worrying about what needed to be done or what time they had to leave the house in the morning. He shoulders dropped as he grabbed a handful of the colorful crayons in front of them. Cami flipped rapidly through the book, as if she were looking for a specific picture.

"This one." Her little hand slapped the page in front of her. Brody peered at it. He stared at the picture of a family standing in front of a barn. Next to the father was a small tractor with eyes for headlights. He bit his lip.

"This is the picture I want to color. And when it's all finished I'm bringing it to Grammy Ruby and Tacy so they can hang it up on their refrigerator. They don't have any pictures on theirs."

The handful of crayons slipped from his hand.

"Daddy, you dropped your crayons."

"That's ok, honey." His hand shook as he grasped at the crayons he'd dropped.

"So can we?"

"Can we what?" A sweaty hand clutched the waxy colored sticks.

"Can we take this picture to Grammy Ruby and Tacy tomorrow?" She cocked her head, a look of exasperation in her eyes.

"Uh, sure. Sure. Tomorrow I'll take you over there after school. You can spend some time with Ruby."

"You're not going to stay? I'll bet they miss you."

Brody tried to control his breathing so as to slow his pounding his heart. He stroked his daughter's yellow locks, his eyes on the fuchsia head band she'd insisted on wearing that morning.

"No, baby. I have to get back to the coffee shop. You go have some fun with everyone. I'll come by and pick you up later on." But even as he said it he was already planning to ask Lucy to give Cami a ride home. He'd have to have a strategy if he planned on avoiding seeing Tacy Clark.

## Chapter Thirteen

The last two days seemed unending to Tacy. Wednesday came and went uneventfully, and she'd felt almost robotic on Thursday as she fell into her routine of getting up, cooking breakfast for her aunt and setting out for the orchards. Lucy hadn't been able to pick but her two brothers, Michael and Peter, had remained a loyal part of her small crew.

Each day was a repeat of the prior one. She'd cook, they'd eat and then sit in the living room. After their emotional breakthrough on Tuesday, there was a new closeness between them, something Tacy felt was almost like a mother-daughter bond.

She'd toyed with the idea of staying behind, feeling tired just thinking of her busy and loud life in the city. She wasn't sure what she would do if she decided to stay in Hill Top. She wasn't a confused twenty year old girl anymore. She'd need to do something with her life and she still wanted to pursue her love of music.

But somehow the strong driving force to be a success in professional music had been tamped down, by what she wasn't quite sure. Though the last two days she'd enjoyed the new relationship and understanding she'd found with her aunt, the highlight of her days had been little Cami's visits.

She tried, but she couldn't hide her disappointment over the fact that Brody chose not to come in to drop off or pick up his little girl. When she saw Lucy, whom she had since begun to rebuild a friendship with, outside waiting to take Cami home on Wednesday, it felt as if she'd been hit in the chest. It was obvious that he had made a mistake kissing her that night under the moon and stars deep in the apple orchards. She tried to reason with herself. They'd both been carried away by the moment. It was the setting, practically the cover of a cheap romance novel, with ripe apples dangling from bending branches, the glow of the moon and twinkling stars. What man and woman wouldn't have ended up kissing as they had? She shouldn't have let it go to her head. She'd already knew that the only person Brody was willing to devote his time and love to was his daughter. She couldn't blame him for that. Instead of acting like a love sick teenager, she needed to figure out what she was going to do about the annual harvest festival.

They'd been picking apples for four days. Granted they were a small crew, but they were in sync with one another. They had all worked hard, only breaking for a quick lunch and occasional sips of water. The teenagers and Lucy's brothers had all put in ten hour days with no complaints. Still, there were more apples on the ground then in the baskets. Once an apple hit the ground it was more than likely bruised and couldn't be put in the baskets to be sold at fruit stands. If they'd been looking for apples for the press to make juice for the festival, it would have been one thing. But Uncle Jerry's apple press hadn't been used since her uncle had taken ill, and she knew one press would never produce enough juice to earn worthwhile sales.

No, they were supposed to come up with bushel upon bushel of apples for the festival, and they couldn't be bruised or banged up in any way. Without enough apples to donate to the festival, she knew the church preschool would not have enough funds to offer full day school to the families who were counting on it. And Cami was one of those kids whose father was counting on it.

An image of Brody came to mind but she swatted it from her thoughts.

Tomorrow would be their last day to pick as much as they could for Saturday's festival. Tacy had resigned herself to the kitchen in the late afternoon while Ruby, who had graduated to a cane, escorted Cami out to the front porch. Picking through the refrigerator for ideas for dinner, Tacy kept one ear tuned toward the front of the house, listening for Lucy and her aunt's chatter. But it was Brody's voice coming from the porch. She closed the refrigerator door and tiptoed to the entryway of the kitchen to hear what they were saying. She stepped into the hall and practically crawled to the living room door. If he looked in through the screen door, he would see her acting like a silly school girl, her body scrunched up against the wall. She strained to hear, almost sure she'd caught her name in their conversation. And then it was quiet. She hurried back to the kitchen and flung open the refrigerator, pretending to be engrossed in plastic containers of leftovers.

"Brody just took Cami home. He said he didn't have time to stop in."

Tacy tried to compose herself. She turned

around and looked at her aunt. Seeing the concern on her aunt's face, she felt a flush of heat.

"Well, he's probably had a busy day at the coffee shop. Thursdays are the start of a busy weekend for small businesses like his." She turned back to the refrigerator and reached in, shuffling bottles and containers around.

"Maybe so, but don't you think you should talk to him? It just seems to me like you two have been avoiding each other. Even little Cami said something to that effect." Her aunt stood up and grabbed the cane from the back of her chair. She hobbled over and touched Tacy's back.

"I see something there, in both of you. He's been such a good neighbor and I wouldn't want to see him hurt. And I know you've been hurt enough too."

Tacy didn't want to hurt her aunt. She eased away from her aunt's hand on her back and walked over to the stove, grabbing the tea kettle and shook it. Still full, she set it on a burner and turned it on.

"Aunt Ruby, it's not what you think. We've just been working together to get the apples picked and ready for Saturday. He's a nice guy, but that's all. He's not interested in anything more than that, and neither am I." She stood beside the stove listening to the hiss of the flames as they licked the bottom of the orange aluminum kettle.

"Tacy, I don't know a lot of what goes on these days. I don't know about the world wide webs or why you young kids are pecking on those phones you carry in your hands all the time, but I do know promise when I see it. Almost fifty years ago I saw it in your uncle and I see it in you and Brody. Why don't you go talk to him?"

"Aunt Ruby, there's nothing to talk about. We already took care of everything for the harvest. He did his share to help out and I'm taking care of the rest. What do we have to talk about?" She turned off the burner. Her aunt was staring at her now, the weight of her body on her good side, a sparkle in her watery blue eyes.

"That's what you need to find out, dear." She hobbled towards the kitchen door and stopped. "I had a late lunch with Cami today so I think I'll skip dinner tonight. Don't worry about me. You're free to do whatever you'd like this evening." She put a finger to her lips, kissed it, and wiggled at Tacy, something her uncle used to do every morning as she left for school.

Tacy felt her eyes well up. She did the same back and watched as her aunt left the room. Glancing at the clock, she imagined Brody and Cami were settled at home now, probably making something to eat. No doubt after dinner they'd spend a little time together before the little girl had to get to bed.

If he'd wanted to talk to her he would have stopped in, wouldn't he?

Feeling agitated, she dumped the steaming hot water from the kettle in the sink. She opened the refrigerator. Nothing had changed since the last two times she'd studied its contents.

She glanced at the clock again. It was a little after seven. She had a long night ahead of her and nothing to do and no one to talk to.

She paced the living room, staring out the big picture window at the infinite darkness. She stared at the path that she'd walked each day for an almost entire week now. She sat down on the big plush ottoman under the window and felt something poke her bottom.

"Ouch." She jumped up and reached down. Cami's plastic giraffe. She'd just shown it to her and Ruby today, beaming with pride that she'd won the prize for being Miss Lizzy's Thursday helper. She must have dropped it while she was packing up her backpack. She fingered the tiny yellow toy. She could always leave it on the kitchen table with a note for her aunt to give it to Cami. But then what if Cami just noticed it was missing? She might be crying for it, disappointed that she wasn't able to show it to her father tonight. The thought of the little girl crying tugged at her. Well, seven o'clock wasn't that late. She could just take a run over to Brody's place and leave it on their welcome mat.

*Oh, that's perfect. Just the right spot for them to step on it and crush it in the morning.*

Okay, okay, she would ring the bell and hand it to Brody. Just to be sure the little girl got it. Nothing more than that.

She hurried to the front door, stopping to grab one of her aunt's sweaters. The evening air had cooled considerably now that it was close to mid-October. She stepped out onto the porch, closing the door quietly behind her. She looked at her Beetle. It was too far to walk, and she'd have to open the noisy garage door if she wanted to use her aunt's car.

Then it dawned on her. She hurried towards the path. Even in the darkness she knew its twists and turns by heart. She only wished she'd thought to bring a flashlight to navigate the barn until she could find the light switch dangling from the ceiling.

Running her hands along the barn doors she found the handles and gave them a great big pull. The darkness almost swallowed her whole, but she pushed past the anxious feeling and swung her hands in the air, latching onto the heavy string attached to the light bulb. With one pull the barn was flooded with light. She looked over at the tractor and smiled. It was better than nothing.

~

Brody Porter had to do a double take. He'd left Cami sitting at the kitchen table coloring as they waited for the noodle casserole to finish cooking in the oven. He'd darted into the living room to grab a few more crayons from her backpack, when he heard the rumbling sound. Ruby was his only neighbor to his left. To his right there was only a wooded area, acres of land that had yet to be developed.

When he'd been looking for a house for the two of them, it had been one appealing aspect of this house. A lot of people would have gone crazy from the constant quiet, but he liked it. He'd had enough experience with noise and city life. This was what he wanted.

The rumbling sound was louder than any truck he'd ever heard, and he pulled open the curtain covering the three boxy windows at the front of the living room.

Replacing those three small squares with a big bay window was on his renovations list. He just didn't seem to have the time. Or the money. But if the preschool got the funding it needed for full day classes, he'd be expanding his menu at the coffee shop and he would be able to continue fixing up this house. He'd make it the homiest home Cami could ever live in.

At first he thought he was imagining things. But as his eyes adjusted from the bright lights of the room to the darkness outside, he knew he wasn't. Tacy Clark was sitting in the seat of the old green tractor, her hands clutching the steering wheel as she pulled into his dirt driveway, rocks kicking up from the thick black tires. He stood in the window, half hidden by the curtain, his feet stuck to the floor. It was his daughter's squeals that snapped him out of the trance-like state.

"Daddy, look!" Cami had not only left her spot in the kitchen, but she had swung the front door wide open and was standing in it, her tiny arms high in the air waving furiously to Tacy.

"Cami! You shouldn't open the door when I'm not with you." He ran over and pulled her tiny body in to the room. He'd told her hundreds of times that she was not allowed to go outside by herself.

"But it's Tacy, Daddy. I wasn't going to be by myself." Like a wiggly puppy, she slipped out of his hands and stomped down the porch steps towards Tacy, who had dismounted from the tractor.

Brody watched her wrap Cami in a big hug. His heart thumping, he ran a hand through his hair. He tried to hide the smile tugging at the corners of his mouth. Now the two were walking slowly towards the porch steps, Cami's hand snug in Tacy's. Cami bounded up the steps and stopped on the porch.

"Come on, Tacy. You're coming inside, right?" Her bright blue eyes darted from Tacy to her father, as if she knew unspoken words were going between the two of them.

Tacy's dark brown eyes looked at him. She looked uncomfortable standing there. Then he watched as she reached into the pocket of the bulky cardigan she was wearing.

"Actually, I just came by to give something to Cami." She pulled out a tiny plastic toy and held it out for him to see, as if she wanted to prove she was just making a quick stop.

"You must have left that at Ruby's house earlier." He spoke to Cami, trying hard not to look into Tacy's warm eyes. He didn't want to make more out of the visit than it was. She'd said herself she had just come by to give the toy to Cami.

"My giraffe! Daddy, that's the prize I told you about that I thought I lost." Cami's sneaker clad feet bounded down the stairs once again, her small hand grabbing the small plastic animal from Tacy's hand. Slipping the toy in her jeans pocket, she latched on to Tacy's hand.

"But you can come inside, right? You can stay, right? I want to show you my room and my stuffed animals. And the chair daddy made for me." The little girl was chattering a mile a minute.

Brody couldn't help but break into a smile. He looked at Tacy and shrugged his shoulders.

"So, I guess you'd better come in. It seems my daughter has a lot of stuff she wants to show you." His smile felt genuine.

For the last four days, he'd plastered on an obligatory smile for his customers as they passed through the shop. A warmth came over him that he was sure had nothing to do with the weather, especially since the nights had cooled significantly.

Tacy smiled back at him and walked up the porch steps. Before Brody could say anything else to her, Cami had dragged her to the door. He followed the two girls inside.

"I was coloring while dinner was getting ready. But we can go see my room and my stuffed animals now." Tacy gave him a nod and let Cami lead her down the hallway to the staircase that led to the bedrooms.

With nothing else to say, he yelled after them as they ran up the steps, "I'll just be in the kitchen."

He peered in the oven door. The casserole was just about ready. He wondered if Tacy had eaten yet. There certainly was plenty to spare if she wanted to stay. He was only thinking of asking her to join them for his daughter's sake. This way she'd have more time to show Tacy all the things she was talking about.

Hearing his daughter's feet running into the kitchen, he turned around and found himself face to face with Tacy.

"Hey, there. Guess you got the grand tour?" Feeling silly wearing the bulky glove potholders, he tossed them on to the counter and walked over to the table. He picked up the crayons and coloring book, dropping them into the basket under the bench against the wall.

"I sure did. You've done a great job on her room. It's the perfect little girl's room."

"Thank you. I tried to channel my inner girl." *Great. Just great. What she must be thinking.* He flushed from head to toe. He turned away from her, pretending to need something from a cabinet.

"She's a lucky little girl."

He turned around to face her, hoping he didn't look as red as he felt.

She stood there, wrapped in what was obviously

her aunt's bulky cardigan, her face flushed whether from the heat of the kitchen or the awkwardness of the situation. The blue and white checked flannel shirt, jeans and brown cowboy boots suited her. A little too well.

"Thank you. I try my best."

He wasn't sure what was smothering him more, the heat of the kitchen or the uncomfortable silence. He wanted her to stay.

"Have you eaten yet? Because we were just getting ready to have dinner and we've got plenty. You're welcome to join us if you can. I mean I don't know if you have to get back to Ruby or if..." His words were getting stuck in his mouth like the peanut butter on bread he made each day for Cami's lunch.

"Oh, no. Aunt Ruby said she had a late lunch with Cami so she wasn't feeling very hungry. I'm free. I'd like to stay." She turned around to look at Cami, who had parked herself in a kitchen chair, her feet tucked underneath her.

It hadn't occurred to him how oddly quiet she'd been.

"So, would you like that Cami? Would you like Tacy to stay for dinner?" He didn't need to ask. Her head bobbed up and down, her yellow curls slipping out from behind the fuchsia headband she had been wearing for days.

"Can I help with anything?" Tacy asked him.

Brody looked around the room.

"You're a guest and I don't put guests to work, but if you wouldn't mind setting the table that would help me out."

He thought he saw her visibly relax, her

shoulders drop just a bit.

"I love setting the table." She turned to Cami. "When I was a little bit older than you, setting the table was one of my chores at home. I loved folding the napkins and setting the forks and knives on them."

He watched his daughter's eyes widen.

"Can you teach me how to fold the napkins like you did when you were a kid?"

"Absolutely. It's very easy and it makes the table look so nice."

Tacy grabbed a napkin from the wooden holder perched in front of the extra chair at the table they never used. Brody tore himself away from the napkin demonstration to get the food ready. He opened the oven door, grabbed a pair of potholders and pulled out the glass casserole dish. He laid the piping hot dish on the counter and opened the refrigerator, grabbing the green salad he'd made early that morning. He turned to grab the salad bowls from the cabinet and bumped straight into Tacy.

"Oh, I'm sorry. We finished our napkins and Cami said the plates were in this cabinet."

She looked as flustered as he felt. He watched her hands carefully pull out three plates. She left the cabinet open for him.

"That's okay. She's my kitchen expert. She knows where everything is. Trouble is, she can't reach these high cabinets and I don't like her climbing."

"Oh, I don't blame you. It's too easy to take a tumble and get hurt. If I had a little kid climbing around in the kitchen I'd be a nervous wreck. I'd have to throw pillows underneath her every time she moved." She grinned at her own words and his heart skipped a beat.

"Sounds like a good plan to me. I hate when she gets hurt. I guess I'm just an overprotective dad."

They were standing just inches apart, her with the plates tucked against her chest, him with the salad bowls dangling in his left hand. He'd almost forgotten Cami was in the room.

"Tacy, come on. Let's set the table so we can eat. I'm starving." Cami's little voice broke their spell.

"I'd better get these to the table. My helper is waiting." She darted away from him and headed for the table, nearly dropping the plates on it.

Worried he might drop something himself, he put the salad bowls on the counter. He reached in the drawer for the serving spoons and uncovered the salad bowl. As Tacy and Cami set the table together, their animated chatter almost musical, he filled each bowl with lettuce and tomatoes. He reached in the refrigerator and grabbed whatever salad dressing he could find. Practicing his waiter skills, he balanced two bowls on his right arm and held the third in his left hand. He left them on the table and hurried back to get the casserole dish.

"So, are we all ready?"

From the arrangement they had made, it seemed he would be sitting to Tacy's left while his daughter said on Tacy's right. It took him back a bit, knowing how Cami insisted on always sitting next to him. Looks like he'd been replaced at the table.

He sat down in the chair next to Tacy and glanced at each of his dinner companions. They looked like a happy little family. The thought unnerved him.

"Let's eat." He was about to dig in when his daughter waved a hand at him.

"Daddy, you forgot grace. We always say grace at dinner." She turned from her father to Tacy.

"Tacy, you can say the grace since you're our guest and that's what we do when we have company Miss Lizzy says."

He saw the startled look in Tacy's eyes. He guessed she didn't say grace too often. He was about to say something to smooth it over for her when she opened her mouth.

"I'd love to. Father, we thank you for this food, for the man who worked so hard to make it for us, and for getting us together tonight." She stopped and looked over at Cami, who stared at her with one eye open.

"And we thank you for plastic giraffes. Amen."

Brody's *amen* came out a little louder than he'd intended.

After dinner they went out to the living room. Tacy tried to insist on helping clean up, but he'd told her to let everything just sit for a moment. He could clean up any time. How often did he have company, as his grandmother would have said. He watched as Cami showed off the wooden rocker he'd made from scratch for her. Tacy ran a finger over the wood, remarking on how fine the finish was. He felt like a rooster with his chest puffed up. They all laughed when Cami invited her to try it and Tacy told her that she was pretty sure if she sat in that chair her father would have to use his carving skills to cut her out of it.

Tacy and Cami sat together on the loveseat, his daughter keeping her attention with all her school chatter and talk about Sunday school friends. It gave Brody time to take Tacy in. His eyes noted all the little things, like the way her eyes twinkled when she laughed, or the way her lips pursed when she was thinking about something Cami had said. He'd been so entranced with her that the buzz of her cell phone made him jump.

"Oh, wow. That can't be Aunt Ruby. She's not a fan of technology." She chuckled as she slipped her phone out of her back pocket. Brody saw her eyebrows arch in surprise.

"Something wrong? Everything okay?" He sat forward on the sofa and waited for her to say something. Seeing her face pale, he was beginning to grow concerned. He had to resist the urge to go over to the love-seat and hold her hand.

"It's...it's my agent. The spot I was going to audition for in two weeks has opened up early. They want me to come audition on Saturday."

Brody held his breath, grateful he hadn't gone over to her after all. Holding her hand would have just made the situation worse. He'd told himself he would never get involved again with a woman younger than himself that was only waiting for the next opportunity to knock. And here he was, heart thumping in his chest, as another woman he had fallen for was telling him she was leaving.

# Chapter Fourteen

Tacy didn't want to take the tractor down into the orchards to help load up the last baskets of apples on Friday afternoon. Using the excuse of having to take care of business details, she had asked Michael to leave the group behind and come pick up the tractor around five o'clock. The memory of her driving home from Brody's the night before was too fresh in her mind. And if she thought she could try to forget the kiss he'd planted on her lips that night in the orchards, she was fooling herself after the sudden forceful kiss he'd given her in the doorway of his home last night.

It was all so confusing. Especially since he'd abruptly ended their night together. They'd been having such a good time together, the three of them, but after that text she'd gotten about the audition everything had changed. All of a sudden he was in a hurry to get Cami to bed. And in even more of a hurry to send Tacy home. He'd shocked her with that kiss and then just as abruptly closed the door behind her as she walked out, not even watching to see that she got on her way. Granted she was only riding the tractor back to the barn. But deep inside she'd almost thought he might have offered her a ride home. She could easily have picked up the tractor in the light of day the next morning.

Lucy hadn't been able to pick with them for the last day, but that was okay. Tacy was thrilled that her old friend was calling her regularly to check in on their progress. Her brothers were a blessing and Tacy was grateful to her for sending them her way. For a small team of three high school kids and two college boys they were doing better than she would have imagined. Still there weren't as many filled apple crates as she had hoped for.

When she'd told Lucy earlier that morning about the text, she'd done what she would have done for Tacy all those years ago when they were best friends. She offered Tacy her car for the weekend. Lucy told her to take her car on Saturday and go for it. She agreed with Tacy that it sounded like the opportunity of a lifetime. The ease of slipping into an old friendship like they'd never parted was something Tacy would never have thought would happen.

All day long she'd been tossing the dilemma around in her head, trying to decide what to do. In just a week's time, she was finding the idea of staying in Hill Top too appealing. The idea of being back home with her aunt and the new wonderful relationship they were enjoying and the comfort of a familiar friend dangled like carrots just out of reach. She tried to tell herself that if she stayed it would have nothing to do with Brody Porter and Cami. But even she didn't believe herself.

She was surrounded by at least a hundred baskets of freshly picked apples. Michael had managed to park the tractor in its usual spot and unhitched the wagon as she had asked. Together they had shook out aprons and hung them up on the barn walls.

"Are you sure you don't need that wagon hitched to the tractor anymore? How are you planning on getting all those baskets to the church for the festival tomorrow?" Michael had a look of doubt on his face.

"Yes, that's fine. The two church custodians are heading over here at six am with the church bus. They can take all the baskets in one trip which I couldn't do with just the wagon. No worries."

He shook his head and walked over to her little crew standing against the beam in the center of the barn, sipping soda and water. Before she forgot, she grabbed the envelopes she'd left on the shelf behind the wagon.

"Jack, Erin, Mary Ellen...I have your week's pay here." She handed each of the high schoolers a white envelope with their promised week's pay.

She turned toward Michael and Peter and held out an envelope for each of them. Peter push the envelopes back at her and shook his head.

"My sister would give us an earful if we took that money. We just wanted to help you out. There's no need to pay us."

Michael was nodding in his head in agreement with his brother.

"I can't, guys. You have to let me give you something. You've worked so hard. I promised anyone who worked a few days' I would pay them, and you earned it too."

The two brothers backed up from her, putting their hands in their pockets. They were both shaking their heads now.

"Okay, well, then I'll find another way to pay you for this. Give me time and I'll come up with something." She blinked back tears threatening and turned to face her small crew of five.

"I just want to say how much I appreciate all the help you've given me this week. You've all worked so very hard and this turned out better than I imagined. I hope you guys get to have some fun at the festival tomorrow."

She made the rounds to each of them, kissing the girls and patting the guys on their backs. And after a few more minutes, all five of them disappeared from her sight. She stood alone holding the two envelopes that had been refused.

There wasn't much left to do in the barn. She walked over to the rows and rows of crates filled with apples and stared at them. She was sure she was forgetting something Uncle Jerry used to do during apple picking season.

The filled to the brim crates sat directly on the barn floor. She wondered if they'd pick up the dust from the ground, then decided probably not.

The tractor was shut down, the wagon close behind it but unhitched. The aprons had been shook out and hung up, ready for the next season that probably wouldn't be. With nothing more to do, she headed out.

For the last time, she threw her might into it and pulled the barn doors shut, dropping the latch across them.

As she stood outside the barn, she noticed the sky looking darker than it had earlier. It didn't look like a typical October sky. *Must be some rain coming.*

As she hurried along the pathway to the house it seemed as if someone had fiddled with the dimmer switch. It was getting darker than usual for six thirty in the evening. The wind caught her wavy locks, blowing them in her eyes and mouth. She swatted her hair away and picked up her pace.

She'd given in to her aunt's pleas to let her make dinner for a change. Her aunt kept saying how hard she was working with the pickers and how she'd love to make something special for Tacy for a change. Feeling spent, Tacy agreed.

Now as she hurried up the porch steps, the scent of something good filled her nostrils. She was grateful she'd taken her aunt up on the offer. Her back was aching, her hands were calloused, and she was just feeling heavy. When she opened the front door, she found her aunt watching the television in the living room. Since she'd been home they hadn't looked at it once, spending their nights instead listening to her aunt's favorite music and playing card games. Seeing her aunt glued to the screen, she sat down on the sofa next to her.

"What's going on?" She asked Aunt Ruby. She watched the reporter on the screen as he pointed to numbers and figures on the wall behind him.

"They're saying we're getting some kind of rain storm. A heavy downpour with possible hail and flooding. That's most unusual for Hill Top, especially in October." Her aunt's lips were taut, a look of concern in her eyes.

"Oh, I wouldn't worry Aunt Ruby. You know how these weather people are. They're always forecasting the end of the world. Half the time they predict heavy rains and we get three drops." She got up off the sofa and headed for the hallway.

"I'm going to take a quick shower and clean up.

What smells so good?"

She'd managed to distract her aunt from the forecast of doom and gloom. Aunt Ruby brightened up and got up, switching off the television and picking up her cane. She followed after Tacy.

"I've got homemade macaroni and cheese and home baked bread for us tonight. I think after all that hard work you need something that'll stick to your bones." She was grinning at Tacy.

Tacy beamed back at her. "That is my all-time favorite. It smells delicious and I'm starving. Give me two seconds and I'll be ready to eat."

She raced down the hall and grabbed the jeans and long sleeve fleece shirt she had washed that morning. She had wanted to make sure she had something cozy to wear after a long week of hard work. With a towel and clothes in hand she headed for the bathroom.

The familiar tub and tiles comforted her as she turned on the shower. She grabbed a shower cap and pulled her hair up, tucking it inside the plastic. She'd wash her hair tomorrow. Right now she just wanted to get the dirt of the day off and enjoy a hot meal. It was the fastest shower she'd ever taken. She'd barely soaped and rinsed and she was out and drying off.

She stepped in to the kitchen to find Aunt Ruby had done everything herself.

"Aunt Ruby, you should have left something for me. I was planning to set the table, since you cooked the meal." She stared at the table already fully set and the small basket of fresh bread in the center.

"Don't be silly. You've done enough already. Let's sit down, dear." Aunt Ruby was standing with a bubbling hot dish of the macaroni and cheese, her cane draped over her arm.

"Wait! You only have two hands. I'll take the dish and you use your cane. I'd rather you not have another fall." Tacy smiled as she grabbed two pot holders and let her aunt pass the hot dish to her. She set it down next to the bread and waited for her aunt to be seated. "This smells so good my nose is telling my stomach to look out." Tacy laughed.

Just as she grabbed the serving spoon the light above their heads flashed.

"What on earth?" Her aunt stared up at the stained glass chandelier. "I can't remember the last time that bulb was changed. Tacy, you might have to go down in the basement and look around for a bulb. I think it's been years since I changed this one."

Tacy cocked her head and stared at the bulb. Just as she was about to say something a bolt of light flashed outside the window, followed by a rumble so loud Tacy swore she could feel the floor move.

"I think that storm really is coming." Aunt Ruby sat up in her chair, craning to see out the window. A torrent of rain ran down the window pane.

"Wow. I guess I shouldn't have doubted the forecast." She thought back to her walk down the path just a short while ago. She should have known – the darkened skies, the gust of wind – she'd completely missed the signs.

"Well, as long as we don't lose power we should be fine, Tacy." Her aunt took a forkful of the creamy macaroni and closed her eyes.

Distracted by the rain relentlessly hitting the window, Tacy held her fork in mid-air. She was remembering, another storm so many years ago during October. Her Uncle Jerry had to rush back to the barn to do something. In her mind she saw it clear as day. The pallets. He'd gone up to the barn to put all the baskets up on pallets because the barn sometimes flooded. And a flood would destroy the harvest.

"Aunt Ruby, I think we might not be fine after all."

She stood up and pushed her chair back, hurrying out of the kitchen. She threw open the closet and sorted through a dozen or more coats that rarely saw the light of day. She recognized Uncle Jerry's old winter coats. She kept pushing the hangers along until she found what she was looking for. Uncle Jerry's rain slicker. They didn't make them like this anymore, a heavy durable rubber complete with hood. She hung it over the door and bent down, searching for the matching boots. They'd swim on her but it was better than apples swimming in the barn.

"Tacy, what are you doing?" Aunt Ruby's frightened face stopped her.

"Aunt Ruby, I just remembered a storm like this when I was about twelve years old. Uncle Jerry had to go out to the barn and get those baskets up on pallets. If the barn floods, the whole harvest will be ruined. I have to get up there." She saw the look of horror cross her aunt's face.

"But Tacy, your uncle had help all those years ago. What can you do all by yourself? And it's dangerous out there. You could get hurt." She was clutching her cane with both hands, bent over in panic.

"Don't worry about me. I can do this. Just promise me you'll stay put so I have one less thing to worry about. I'll be back as soon as I'm done."

As she opened the door a gust of wind and rain threatened to rip it out of her hands. She held on tight and lowered her head against its force.

"Tacy, please...don't go. This is a bad idea."

"Aunt Ruby, don't worry. I'll be fine. I promise. Just stay inside and wait for me." Before her aunt could say another word she was running down the steps and heading for the path, wishing she'd thought to bring a flashlight once again.

~

For the last hour, Brody had been fighting the urge. He was trying his best to stay occupied with various games and adventures Cami kept dreaming up for the two of them. Outside the torrential sheets of rain were flooding the driveway and grass. The last time he'd checked, the water was beginning to creep up the tires of his pickup, never a good sign.

After a couple of rounds of lights flickering throughout the house, he'd gotten a few flashlights from the closet just to be on the safe side. Surprisingly, Cami wasn't very unnerved about the storm. He'd half expected her to be clinging to him when the lights began to flicker. She'd never been afraid of the dark, but between the flickering and bouts of roof shaking thunder he'd thought for sure she'd be looking to climb on his lap for shelter. They were setting up their fourth game of Candy Forest when she spoke what he'd been trying not to think about all evening.

"Do you think Tacy and Grammy Ruby are okay?" Her bright blue eyes were all business as she waited for him to answer.

His right hand clutched his bearded chin, a habit

he'd taken to any time he was deep in thought or about to make a decision on something.

"Well, I'm sure they're very happy about this storm, but if we've got lights, then they've got lights. I'm sure they're fine." He started dealing cards from the small deck that came with the game.

"But it's flooding outside. I looked out the window and it looks deep. What if they can't get out of the house?" She persisted, her small hand tugging his shirt sleeve.

"Honey, on a night like this Ruby...Grammy Ruby and Tacy are probably not going anywhere."

For a moment, he wondered if she'd still been in the barn when the storm started. No, most likely she'd been home by then. He knew the crew stopped working once they lost daylight. She must have been home when the rain started. And since Ruby had lived in the old farmhouse her whole life, he was sure she had plenty of flashlights on hand.

It occurred to him that she might not have batteries though. She'd been living alone for several years. Picking up batteries was a man's job. When was the last time she'd gotten batteries for her flashlights? He'd never brought her any himself and he'd been in town for over two years.

His mind began churning away, but he refused to let his thoughts get the best of him. More than likely Tacy had found some batteries lying around and had taken care of them herself.

"Don't you think we ought to go see if they're all right?" Cami pushed away the board game and plopped herself in the spot where'd they been playing.

She was sitting cross legged in front of him, her

arms propped up on her knees and her chin resting on tiny balled up fists.

"Honey, it's pretty bad out there. I don't even think we should attempt to go out until the rain stops. I'm sure they're fine."

"Can I call Grammy Ruby and ask her myself?"

He could see that until she got what she wanted she wasn't going to let up. He nodded his head and pointed to the table top phone he'd had installed when they'd moved in. Back in Chicago most people he knew had removed their land lines, opting for their cell phones instead. But here in Hill Top most folks still had at least one land line in their homes. He'd found it comforting, like an old memory of his grandmother and the rotary phone on her kitchen table that, as a child, he'd loved to randomly dial, just to hear the sound the dial made as it went around the face of the phone.

Cami picked up the receiver. Her small finger pointed at the index card next to the phone where he'd written down emergency numbers just in case. Most of the time he was at home with her or she was out somewhere with someone taking care of her so the emergency contact list seemed foolish. But it made him feel like he'd done all he could to protect his little girl.

"Do you need help?" He asked, already knowing she'd refuse it.

"Nope." Her small fingers tapped out the number, but the look on her face made him sit up.

"What's the matter, honey?" His heart picked up in pace.

"I don't hear anything. There's no ringing or nothing." She was holding the receiver up in the air as if he could listen from where he was. Brody pulled himself up from the floor, rubbed his knees and walked over to the table. He took the receiver from her hand and put it to his own ear. Dead silence. The phone was dead. Worry trickled through his mind like the beginnings of a leaky ceiling, slowly going from a droplet to a steady trickle of water.

"Oh, well. That does happen in a storm. That just means the lines are down. I could try my cell phone..." His words died on his lips. He'd never asked Tacy for her cell phone number and with Ruby not owning one there was no way for him to get in touch with either of them. He turned and looked out the living room window. Darkness blanketed the front yard as water teemed down the panes of the picture window. A bolt of lightning lit up the sky, the zigzag looking like it reached down to the ground.

"Get your coat on, Cami. We're heading for Grammy Ruby's house."

Mother Nature's lightning show intermittently lit up the sky, guiding them in the heavy rains as they made the short trip to Ruby's house. Brody's pickup splashed through the flooded driveway as he pulled up as close to the porch as he could. He instructed Cami not to get out, and instead to wait for him to get her. She was delighted to be carried up the stairs to Ruby's front door like a special delivery. When he knocked on the door his heart skipped a beat when Ruby alone answered. He cut to the chase.

"Where's Tacy?" The anxious feeling in his gut made him breathless.

"Oh, Brody! She's gone to the barn to take care of the apples. She's worried they'll be damaged if the barn floods. I've been sitting here worried sick about her." Without a word, he put Cami on the floor, giving her a push towards Ruby, and hurried down the steps, seeing Ruby and his daughter huddled together in the doorway as they watched him pull away.

As he sped down the path he'd cleared for her to get back and forth to the barn all week, his mind raced with all kinds of terrible thoughts. A tree or branch could have come down on her. She could have fallen in the dark inside the barn and hit her head. What was she thinking? How stupid could that woman be?

He leaped out of the truck into a muddy mess, the normally dusty dirt out front of the barn was a mud puddle from the torrential rains. Seeing both barn doors opened he stepped into a half foot of water. His eyes frantically searched the barn when he caught site of a yellow vision behind the tractor.

"Tacy! Tacy, what are you doing?" He waded through the water and grabbed her, wrapping her in his soaking wet arms.

"Brody! I'm trying to save the apples. I've got the pallets set up. I need to get the baskets up out of the water so we don't lose the apples for the festival tomorrow. We'll lose everything without them being up." She wiggled like a little child in trouble, trying to get out of his clutches.

"Not everything." He tried to pull her close, but she slipped out of his arms. "Let me help you. You can't do this alone. You can't do everything in life alone."

With a strength that surprised himself, he started hauling up baskets one after the other, the rain leaking from the roof dripping in his eyes. He watched Tacy as she continued to press on, water running down her face, sloshing in her boots as she maneuvered the baskets on to the pallets.

"Tacy!" He was shouting to get her attention over the thunder and the thud of baskets as she dropped them on to the pallets.

"What?" She yelled over the ground shaking noise.

"Please, don't go. Please don't leave tomorrow." The next thing he knew she was falling onto him in a dead faint.

## Chapter Fifteen

Brody would have rather been over at Ruby's house, checking in on Tacy after her fainting spell, instead of standing in the enormous half paved lot behind the community church. After getting her to come to, holding her in his arms while sitting on the edge of a pallet, he'd ignored her protests and driven her back to Ruby's in his pickup truck. The water had begun to recede, but he'd carried her up the porch steps and into the front door that Ruby had left unlocked.

He'd never forget the look of horror on Ruby's face as he'd lain Tacy down on the sofa. She'd been so upset she'd scurried over, her cane barely touching the floor, and had nearly toppled onto Tacy. He'd been so concerned about Tacy he'd almost forgotten Cami.

He'd kneeled on the floor beside Tacy as she lay on the sofa, holding her cold wet hand. It was then that he'd felt his little girl against him, her eyes looking bigger than robin eggs, and he realized his little girl was crying. He'd pulled her against his side with his free arm and kissed the top of her head, telling Ruby he was pretty sure Tacy was okay, just maybe working too hard on too little in her stomach.

Now as he walked from booth to booth, waving and greeting the local vendors, he wished once again he'd gotten Tacy's cell phone number from Ruby. He just wanted to know if she was okay. He wasn't even sure she was still in Hill Top. She'd never responded to his outburst, his plea for her to skip the audition and stay. He knew he had no right to ask anything of her, but the words had come running out of his mouth as rapidly as the water had been rising in the barn.

He wanted to say more. He wanted to tell her that he'd been grappling with these feelings since they'd talked in his coffee shop. After all the heart ache Carrie Ann had put him through, he knew he must be crazy. But there was something about Tacy, something vulnerable and kind, that had touched a part of his heart he had been sure was locked tight. It had to be real because he saw the way she affected his daughter. He didn't know what he expected to come of it, but he wanted to find out. He was being foolish. He didn't have any idea how Tacy felt about him.

"Hey, Brody, got a coffee booth here today?"

Zeke Williams was standing in front of the booth Brody had reserved for himself for the day, his thumbs twiddling his trademark suspenders. Seeing the man's snow white long beard reminded Brody of his own beard, which was in need of a little grooming at the barber shop as soon as he had the time.

"Sure do, Zeke. I've only got one machine with me here today, so it's going to be a basic kind of day, but I'm introducing some new pastries that I'll be featuring in the shop soon. You ought to come by one day and take a look around."

Zeke Williams was the town die hard. Stuck in the good old days, he was the last to try anything new or, as he called it, newfangled. That included Brews & Bites, Brody's coffee shop, and a first for the small town of Hill Top. He'd become a favorite spot for most people working in or living in Hill Top. But not Zeke Williams. Zeke Williams was going to stick to the coffee bean grinder he'd inherited from his great-granddaddy. And he was going to make his own coffee every morning just like his father, his grandfather, and his great grandfather had done all those years ago.

"Don't need no fancy pants coffee." Zeke's eyes roamed the dome covered cake dishes Brody had been setting up all morning long, lingering on a pomegranate danish sprinkled with confectioners' sugar and a peppermint leaf. Brody smiled.

"Like to try that one, Zeke? It's a pomegranate danish with a peppermint leaf. Cami says it's pretty darned good." He lifted the dome and was about to reach for it when the old man waved a hand at him.

"Pomegranate! What kind of Danish is that? Give me a good old prune Danish any day." And with that Zeke ambled away, thumbs dipping back on to his suspenders.

Brody laughed aloud and gently dropped the dome on to the cake dish. Sighing, his eyes scanned the beginnings of a crowd. Men, women, couples and children were beginning to mill about, eagerly perusing the tables to see what goodies would be for sale this year. On the far side of the grounds, a huge tent had been set up and beneath it were three big bins filled with apples. Brody had gone over to the tent earlier, scoping out the condition of Tacy's apples. He had noticed that Tacy must have given the men a few dozen baskets for people interested in buying an entire bushel of apples. Otherwise, there'd been several piles of plastic bags donated by Dunley's Mini Mart for shoppers to fill with their apples.

It appeared their hard work last night during the downpour had been a worthwhile effort. Everything was in place for the big day. Everything but Tacy Clark. He'd been hoping she would have decided to stay and possibly man the apple booth for the day. Instead, two of the church ladies were standing alongside the bins, smiling happily as they called to festival goers to come in and pick some fresh apples.

Because he'd slept so fitfully the night before, he'd done something in the early hours of the morning that he would be ashamed to ever let anyone know. Sneaking out an hour before he needed to leave, leaving Cami sleeping soundly in her bed, he'd zipped over to Lucy's house, more than a mile past his own home, and checked her driveway.

Lucy had told him during her shift at the coffee shop yesterday that she'd offered Tacy the use of her car to get back to the city in time for the audition. If the car was in the driveway then he'd be leaning toward believing that maybe Tacy had changed her mind. Maybe she'd felt that something between them that he was feeling. If the car was gone, then he had to come to terms with the fact that she'd decided to go back to the city and go through with the audition.

His asking her to stay last night was something he hadn't planned on. He'd promised himself he would never ever beg a woman to stay with him again. He would never again be said to be the guy that had held a woman back from what she wanted. If what Tacy wanted more than anything else was that shot at the orchestra in New York City, he wasn't going to hold her back. If he was going to commit his life – and his daughter's - to a woman, it was going to be to a woman who wanted him first and foremost, before anything else.

He was driving himself crazy. He'd seen Lucy's empty driveway with his very own eyes. She had left sometime this morning. She'd made her decision. Now he had to forget about her and get on with his life. He'd been fine, more than fine, living in Hill Top before she'd come back. He'd be fine again. Picturing his little girl's disappointed face when she found out Tacy had left, was the only thing that made his heart ache more than it did already. He'd never ever let that happen again.

"Brody!" Mrs. Hansen, a church elder, was perusing his table, her eyes flitting from one pastry to the other. "Everything here looks so tempting."

"Well, I have a few pastries I'll be cutting up for samples. Why don't you come back in a few minutes and you can sample something?"

He smiled at the way her fingers pointed from one treat to another. This was the beginning for him. If his new pastries and treats were a hit at the annual harvest festival, he was sure they'd be a hit in his shop. And that would naturally help him introduce a lunch menu, one he'd been planning for months.

The whole plan hinged on just one thing - the apples bringing in enough money for the church to make the preschool an all-day operation. Judging from the apples sitting under the tent on the far side of the grounds, he had a good feeling.

"That's very sweet. I'll do that." She walked away and headed for his neighbor.

Brody eyed the back door of the church. The

door led to the church basement, and today several of the teenage girls from the youth group were running a mini day camp for the children of vendors or parents who just wanted to enjoy the festival on their own. Cami was all too happy to go downstairs this morning when he'd pulled up ready to set up his booth. Several of her Sunday school friends were already running about when he'd left her down there.

Since Lucy and her husband had a repairman scheduled to come in for their burner today, he'd decided to run his booth on his own. With only a few drinks to sell and a limited number of pastries, he was sure he'd be able to handle the customers he attracted.

He pulled out a foil pan with another of his sweet treats and grabbed a knife to cut them up. He'd offer some as samples and some for sale. Behind him his coffee machine hummed away. He'd purposely picked a spot close enough to a pole with a power outlet, knowing he'd need electricity to run his booth.

On each side of him, vendors were set up and chatting with customers. He knew both ladies from town; one the owner of a yarn shop and the other a local crafter who he was told created wire jewelry to sell at all the church bazaars.

*No competition there.*

Hours had gone by and his pastries had been a hit. He was down to just a pan of dark chocolate hazelnut brownies and a few pomegranate Danishes. It was after five o'clock and he was slowly packing it in. He would have left an hour ago, but he wanted to stay around to the end when they announced the total amount of the money the apples had earned for the church preschool. He personally didn't know the amount needed, but he was sure if the needed amount was hit, there would be whooping from the festival committee and church elders. With most everything he'd brought with him back in boxes, he was about to start hauling it all to his pickup truck when he spied Lucy Aimes heading towards him. He gave her a big wave and slipped out from his booth.

"How'd it go for you today?" Her eyes scanned the table, noting that most everything had been packed up and boxed. Her expression was one big question, not sure whether to take the boxes as a good or bad sign.

"Great! It was a really good day. The new stuff was a hit. Well, except for Zeke Williams." He saw Lucy laughed at his mention of the name.

"That's nothing new. But I'm glad to hear you did well. Guess we'll be serving more food this fall, right?" She braced a hand across her forehead, shielding her eyes from the late day sun.

He frowned as he thought about what she'd said.

"That depends on how well the apples did." They looked over in unison, staring at the big tent with the apple bins dwindling down.

"I know you're worried about the preschool money. Tacy really worked hard at it. She did her best. The crew worked hard. I feel like she really cared about raising that money for the school."

He nodded his head. He believed that too. That's what made it hurt worse. He'd seen how once she'd gotten past her anger over the email he'd sent to her masquerading as her aunt that she'd come to care about the preschool. It was Cami. He could see she'd taken a liking to his daughter and she'd wanted to raise enough money for the preschool to offer full day classes. An image of a soaking wet Tacy flashed before his eyes. Why else would she have put herself in harm's way last night, fighting the rain and braving the dark to get those apples to higher ground?

"I know. I saw it myself." He stopped talking and looked away from Lucy. He wanted to ask her the one question that had been tumbling through his mind all day long.

"So, I guess she took your car this morning to make it to that audition?" He felt a zapping pain in his chest as the words came out.

Lucy shot him a questioning look, her eyebrows arched together.

"My car? My car is here in the lot on the other side of the church. She never showed up this morning. The keys I left hidden under the mat on the passenger side were still there when I got in it after the repairman left today."

Brody felt his pulse quicken. She hadn't left? She was still in Hill Top? Had she stayed because he'd asked her to? Or because she'd wanted to before he even asked? Just as he was about to grab Lucy and hug her, out of the corner of his eye he spotted a vision in blue jeans and boots. Never had anything looked as good as Tacy Clark did as she strolled on to the festival grounds.

~

She'd been heading for the big canvas tent where the custodians, Joe and Bill, had told her she could find her apples set up and ready for sale. She was just about ready to step under the shade of the tent when she spotted a big sign, Brews & Bites, in her peripheral vision. Brody's booth. She'd turned to see

Brody and Lucy Aimes chatting in front of the coffee booth. Seeing the boxes on the table and at Brody's feet she guessed that he was done for the day.

Still embarrassed over her fainting spell last night, she was thinking of slipping behind an apple bin when Lucy's waving arm caused Brody to turn and spot her. With nowhere to hide, she waved back. When Lucy's hand pointed to her and then the booth, she knew she was cooked. She cut through the crowds and made her way to Brody's booth, standing awkwardly beside her old friend and the man she wasn't sure what to do about.

"I was wondering if you were going to stop in and check on your apples." Lucy grabbed her and gave her a squeeze.

She squeezed back and looked at Brody, who was staring at her like he hadn't seen her in a long time.

"Yeah, uh, I wanted to be here when they announced whether the church met their goal for the preschool. Aunt Ruby would have come, but she was kind of worn out from last night..." She let the words fade out, remembering that Brody had been there last night and knew more about what had happened than she would have liked.

"Tacy..." Brody began, but the sound of someone banging on a microphone pierced her ears. A rush of static came across the speakers strategically hung from a handful of poles.

"Ladies and gentleman, can we have your attention? Can everyone hear me?" Mrs Hansen, with the same bouffant she'd worn for the last forty years, was yelling into the microphone. It was enough to get everyone's attention.

Men and women stopped talking, mothers pulled on their restless children, and even the teenagers stopped long enough to have a listen.

"As you all know, it's time to announce the results from our fundraiser. This year we've been blessed to have apples donated from Hill Top Orchards. Some of you may have met Tacy, Ruby Clark's niece, who was kind enough to come home and harvest apples to help raise money for our preschool."

Tacy's eyes darted to Brody, wondering if he'd caught the woman's words about her being kind enough to come home. She would have laughed if she didn't feel so uncomfortable.

"Anyway, without further ado, let's get right to business. In my hands I have the amount on a slip of paper. From the looks of these empty bins I'm hopeful that our preschool will be able to, for the first time, offer families in town the first year of full day classes."

Tacy watched the woman fumble with a piece of paper that had been folded what seemed like a hundred different times. She held it up to her eyes, but instead of a smile, she chewed her top lip thoughtfully.

"Everyone, we've made wonderful progress with this fundraiser, but I believe we will have to work a little harder to reach the amount the church needs to offer full day classes..."

A collective round of sighs filled the air. Tacy felt her heart sink. After all she'd been through last night it hadn't been enough after all. She'd had a feeling, but she'd still been optimistic. She glanced at Brody. Seeing the look of disappointment on his face nearly broke her heart. She was about to say something when a man's voice came over the microphone.

"Folks, if I might interrupt..."

Tacy strained to see his face. She knew so many people in Hill Top, and this man was not familiar. She watched as Brody stood at attention, craning to look at the man.

"Brody? Do you know him?" She whispered, not sure he could hear her.

"My name is John Hatcher. Most of you won't know me, but I'm the great-grandson of Elias Hatcher, a long time Hill Top resident. A week or so ago, I came to town. Most of you know my great-grandfather was somewhat of a recluse."

Murmurs spread throughout the crowd. Captivated, Tacy kept her eyes on the man in the dapper suit.

"Anyway, about a month or so ago, my family took my great- grandfather home to be with them. He passed away shortly after. In his will he had specific orders about what he wanted to do with his savings. It wasn't much, but he wanted it donated to the church. I came here today hoping that his donation might help, and from the sounds of it, I think it will. I think my great-grandfather would be happy to know that he helped the preschool reach its goal."

He stepped away from the microphone, handing it back to Mrs. Hansen. Tacy watched as the misty eyed woman hugged the man as he handed her a check. They shook hands as cameras in the crowd snapped pictures followed by enthusiastic clapping.

Tacy was staring at Brody now as the crowd continued to clap. Lucy looked from one to the other, patted Tacy's arm gently, and wandered off to find her husband.

"Wow. That was some shock." It was all she could think of to say. Her heart was pounding wildly against her rib cage and she wondered if the crowd hadn't been making so much noise if Brody would have heard it.

He turned to face her, a soft look on his face.

"Yes, it sure was. I knew I'd seen that guy before. He came in to the coffee shop the same day you did, right before you came in. I knew he wasn't from around here and then he asked for directions for Elias' house. I was wondering what he was up to, but then with everything that was happening I kind of forgot." He inched closer to her. She didn't back away.

"Brody, I didn't come here just to find out about the apples. I wanted to talk to you. I know I didn't answer you last night when you asked me to stay. I was just overwhelmed. Of course it didn't help that I was on an empty stomach." She grinned at him. "But I was so surprised. I know how important Cami is to you and I don't blame you. That's the way a father should be. I wish I'd had a dad like that when I was a little girl. But I remember you saying how she was the love of your life. And I just don't want to be competing with Cami for your love. I've already been an afterthought before. I promised myself I would dedicate myself to my music years ago because I just didn't want to get hurt." She stopped talking to catch her breath. It didn't sound right to her own ears. She wanted to say so much, but somehow it was coming out all confused and garbled.

"Tacy, I love Cami with all my heart. She's a part of me. She's my little girl forever. But when I said she was the love of my life, I wasn't counting on falling in love with you. And it doesn't mean my heart isn't big enough to love you too. I'll confess. I had made a vow that I would never ever fall in love with a woman that was just parking herself until the next big opportunity showed up. I've already been hurt, and I wasn't going to take a chance ever again. And I wasn't going to let anyone hurt Cami like that either. I was protecting my heart and my little girl."

He reached out a hand to her and she took it, his firm grip making her feel protected.

"The only trouble is by sealing up my heart from hurt ,I found out I was missing out on something that makes me feel so wonderful. Someone who makes me feel like I haven't felt in a long time. And last night I finally made up my mind that I didn't want to miss out on a chance to be in love again."

Her pounding heart was now soaring. Tacy couldn't help herself. She dropped his hand and threw herself into him, wrapping her arms around his body, nuzzling her face against his bearded chin.

"I would never hurt you, Brody. I would never hurt Cami. I...I love you. I love Cami. I never answered that text."

She felt his arms squeeze her tighter, his head pressed against the top of her head. His lips brushed her hair. Then he released her from his grip, pushing her gently back so they were face to face.

"Tacy Clark, you are like no other woman I have ever known. I think I fell in love with you at your aunt's dining room table. And I think we're going to have a lot of Saturday evening pizza parties to look forward to."

She stared up into his eyes and before she could say another word, his lips were locked tight on hers and there was no need to talk about anything else.

## The End

"Bloom where you're planted" - Christina's favorite quote

Christina started writing as a young teen, jotting stories in wire ring composition notebooks. Her first typewriter made it faster to get all those stories out of her head and down on paper. Her love of writing has sustained her through a myriad of jobs that included hairdresser,legal secretary, waitress and door-to--door saleswoman.

Luckily for her, writing proved to be successful and a lot less walking than going door to door. SnowGlobe Reunion, a Christian Christmas romance, is Christina's third book. She is also the author of A Husband for Danna and its sequel, A Wife for Humphrey. She is busy working on a fall 2016 release for Forget Me Not Romances. Christina is a member of Romance Writers of America and American Christian Fiction Writers. When she isn't writing or reading, she can be found walking her dog, talking to her herd of cats and spending time with her family.
You can visit Christina's website at:
www.christinalorenzen.com or her Facebook author page
at https://www.facebook.com/ChristinaLorenzenAuthor /